About the Author

Sandy Howe Thompson was born and raised in a small town in the Mississippi Delta. After her high school graduation, she attended Mid-America Baptist Theological Seminary in Memphis, Tennessee. Her husband, Gary, and she had married thirty-seven years ago. She was an executive assistant for thirty years. She is retired. Some of her hobbies are reading, writing, quilting, horseback riding, doll collecting, sewing, designing flower arrangements, interior design, and selling vintage jewelry online.

Delta Daze

Sandy Howe Thompson

Delta Daze

Olympia Publishers
London

www.olympiapublishers.com
OLYMPIA PAPERBACK EDITION

A CIP catalogue record for this title is
available from the British Library.

ISBN: 978-1-80074-377-9

This is a work of fiction.
Names, characters, places and incidents originate from the writer's
imagination. Any resemblance to actual persons, living or dead, is
purely coincidental.

First Published in 2023

Olympia Publishers
Tallis House
2 Tallis Street
London
EC4Y 0AB
Printed in Great Britain

Dedication

I dedicate this book to my mother, Emma Alice Howe. Mama was the best Christian I have ever known. She lived to serve others.

Acknowledgements

I acknowledge my husband, Gary, who never once told me that I was wasting my time writing this book. On the contrary, he encouraged me, in every way, to make *Delta Daze* a reality. Not only he is the love of my life, but he is also my best friend. I acknowledge my parents, the late Earl and Emma Alice Howe. It was because of their unconditional love, country raising on our small Delta farm, and all of the stories told by them, that *Delta Daze* could come to life in a book. I acknowledge my dear sister, Peggy Ann Howe Morgan. I thank her for listening and listening to my book. Moreover, I appreciate our bonded relationship of unconditional love and understanding. I acknowledge three of my beloved nieces, Dorothy Jean Mauro, Barbara Rees and Wanda Joyce Caldwell. Due to the encouragement and inspiration given by them, I had the courage to live my dream and write a book. In particular, Barbara Rees is a great inspiration to me. We played, dreamed, laughed together, and are bonded in a forever love.

Chapter One

Another Sleepy, Dusty, Delta Day

It was the 3rd of June, another sleepy, dusty, Delta day. The old jukebox loudly played the Bobbie Gentry song, *Ode to Billie Joe*, as a tall, slender, dark-haired beauty named Delta strolled past the candy counter at McDonald's Country Store. Everybody knew the song and were always speculating about what was thrown off the Tallahatchie bridge. Right now, that did not matter to Delta for she was more interested in someone outside.

She could hear the rumble of an engine distinctly known by the ears of anybody from these parts as Bill Lawson's old farm truck. Bill was known for his bad reputation, mainly due to his fast driving, cursing and smoking. He was what some would call wild but for Delta, there was something about him that drew her in.

Maybe it was his coal black hair that brushed across his forehead or his muscles that were etched in detail beneath his white t-shirt. Whatever the case, it was something that Daddy would most assuredly disapprove of, especially since he was five years older than Delta. Little did she realize in just a few years how their lives would spin out of control. So begins the story of Delta Daze.

The screen door slammed behind me as I left the store,

just hoping that I would get a glimpse of Bill, or, more importantly, that he would take notice of me. That would not be the case. He only continued to tinker with something under the hood. Oh well, there was plenty of time to work on gaining his attention; after all, I was only sixteen years old.

Seeing the dark cloud building from the southwest gave me an uneasy feeling. I enjoyed walking in the gentle rain, even without an umbrella. However, I knew this rain would be severe, not to mention the lightning, so I hurried home.

Home was a four-room country house located just three miles from Dubbs, Mississippi. For years there was no running water to the house so a pump was used to provide water. In 1957, Daddy, with the help of two of his sons-in-law, added a kitchen which had a sink and the convenience of running water. Nonetheless, there was no hot water, only cold. The outhouse was built some hundred yards away from the house. The placement of the old country farmhouse seemed unquestionably planned, for it sat right smack dab in the middle of forty acres of rich Delta land. She guessed that was the reason her Daddy named her Delta. Living in this house on this land was what she knew, with only the occasional trip to Tunica and Memphis — for that matter — it was mainly what the Daze family had known.

Daddy was a tall, slender man with gray hair around the sides, with a tuft of hair on top. He took no prisoners when it came to discipline. Both of his girls knew just from a look exactly what he was saying, without a word ever being spoken. Delta thought the absolute world of him. It was for his approval that she seemed to take her every breath.

Mama was a well-spoken gentlewoman with a soft southern drawl. Folks from many counties thought the world of her. She loved going to church. She was a member at a small country church, the Berea Baptist Church. Berea had many faithful members. She loved to make certain that her two girls attended regularly. She could not drive, so Daddy always had to drive them there and come back to pick them up. Daddy believed that the church was just made up of a bunch of hypocrites, so it was only during spring and fall revivals that Mama could persuade him to go at least once; even then he would sit outside. Both Daddy and Mama were hard workers. Farming was what they knew and to be a good farmer took a lot of hard work.

Then there was Delta's older, by three years, sister, Peggy. Learning came very easy for Peggy. As a matter of fact, one time in high school, Peggy made one B on her report card. Delta could remember that well for Peggy cried and cried about the grade. Delta, on the other hand, was tickled pink to see a B on her report card and prayed just to reach a passing grade most of the time. Peggy was a brilliant student; there was never any question about that. One day, Peggy will most likely be valedictorian at graduation. Not only is she smart but she is beautiful. How did she get so lucky? I love my sister and looked up to her with great admiration.

I have observed that Peggy has been dating two handsome guys. Without her knowledge, of course, sometimes I have tried to listen to what they say to each other while they are at the door. I love to watch them kiss. Oh, if she knew I had done these things, she would kill me right on the spot. She holds her mouth slightly open; sometimes I see the guy place his tongue into her mouth. Yuck! I just look forward to the day that Daddy will approve of me dating someone, hopefully, Bill, my dreamboat!

Where had the time gone? It was 1962 when the country was enjoying having a young family in the White House. There were nuclear attack advisories at the time, yet this seemed worlds away for Delta.

Mama was ironing and listening to her favorite soap opera, *As the World Turns*, broadcasting from the radio. I was gazing out the bedroom window, watching the fluffy clouds float peacefully by. I had managed to convince Mama earlier that I just did not feel good enough to go to school, all along knowing I was not sick.

I could see puffs of gray smoke coming from the pipes on top of the old John Deere tractor, coming down the side road from a field we called 'The New Ground', which could only mean one thing, Daddy was coming home for dinner. I ran out the front door, just hoping I could catch him before he could get into the yard. On occasion, Daddy would stop the tractor and let me sit in his lap to steer it home. I never grew too old for this, even at sixteen. I was hoping this was one of those times, and it was. I grabbed onto the finder and Daddy gently pulled me up.

"Watch out for that wheel," was always the warning. As I held that big steering wheel, I felt on top of the world!

"Are you feeling better?" Daddy asked as he lifted his cap to wipe the sweat back from his forehead. "It should be unlawful for it to be this hot in May," he continued. That was okay by me for I truly did not want to answer, but I knew it was for the best that I did.

"I guess," I sheepishly replied, knowing Daddy knew me better than anyone, so how could I be fooling him? The truth was, I wasn't.

"Do you think maybe a ride into Dubbs would make you feel any better?" he asked as he stepped off the tractor.

"How am I going to tell Mama?" For I knew that Mama could be a tough cookie if she so chose to be.

"Oh, you let me take care of that. Go put on some shoes and meet me at the truck."

How could I have been blessed with such a great Daddy? I wondered this as I hurried toward the house.

"Bill is going to meet me in Dubbs," Daddy continued.

"Bill who?" I asked.

"Lawson," Daddy replied, as if I should have known. Daddy and Bill were good friends. Maybe Daddy understood him better than most, but I still wasn't sure what would be his reaction to know some of the thoughts that ran through my head. Heaven knows, that could not be! Why, these thoughts I would not even share with my best friend in the whole wide world, Barbara, much less Daddy!

"You run on over to the mercantile store," Daddy instructed, reaching into his pocket to give me a dime.

He knew this would be enough for a cold drink and a candy bar, which was fine by me. I just wished he would let me stay around for a little while after Bill arrived, but I certainly did not know how to bring up that subject without sending up red flags to Daddy. So, I just did as I was told and decided that I would return to the truck before Bill had a chance to leave. Daddy would not question that.

Sure enough, I heard Bill's truck coming, seeming like it was a mile away. It was only at that time that I questioned how in the world I looked.

"Mr. Maynard, do you mind if I use your facilities?" I asked. I could feel my cheeks blushing red!

"Sure can, child," was his reply, scarcely looking up from stocking the shelves.

I combed through my hair, straightened my skirt and put on just a hint of lipstick, just enough, hopefully, that Daddy would not notice.

"Thank you, Mr. Maynard, I will see you next time." The old screen door rattled as it shut behind me and I headed off towards the truck.

I could feel my heart racing. I had not even given a thought as to what I would say. How dumb was I? I slowed my pace down to a stroll.

"Daddy, I am back," I said, acting as though Bill was not even there.

"Delta, I have raised you better than that, can't you even say hi to Bill?" Daddy questioned.

"Why, Bill Lawson, if it isn't you? How are you? Sorry, I guess my mind was elsewhere," I replied, trying my best not to appear nervous. Bill stood back from the truck as if to see exactly who was talking to him. Oh, my, gosh, I don't believe I have ever looked into eyes like those before! They were stark ravening beautiful. I felt like a mute. What should I say? Thoughts were running through my head, but nothing was coming out of my mouth.

"Did you find out what was wrong with the truck?" I gasped, looking for something, anything to say.

"I believe so. Didn't I see you the other day at McDonald's Store out at the Two-Mile-Lake Road?" he questioned. It felt like my heart skipped a beat. He had noticed me.

"Yes, I believe you are right. I could not stop talking due to the thunderstorm coming. I needed to hurry home."

"Oh, that's all right. I kind of figured you were in a hurry," Bill responded, and then went back to what he was doing. I closed the door to the truck.

After returning home, I had thoughts of Bill Lawson running all over my brain. I had to snap out of this or someone, most likely Sister — that is the name I called Peggy — was going to try and put two and two together but I knew it would not add up to Bill. She was smart but not that smart. But I had better not chance it, so I reached for my literature book in an effort to get some homework done. At least, if a nosy Sister walked in, I would look busy. School was almost out for the year and I needed to put a little more effort into my grades anyway.

Chapter Two

The Lawson Family

Lawrence Lawson and his wife, Elizabeth, also known as Liz, had inherited a sizable amount of acreage just outside the town of Dundee. He was a veteran of World War II and his family had come out of the Great Depression with more money than most.

Lawrence's father, William, used his money wisely and bought a fifteen-hundred-acre tract of rich Delta land shortly after 1939. Some of the land had already been cleared, but it was not long until William had all but about fifty acres cleared. His many crops were cotton and soybeans. He also owned a herd of horses.

William was married to a well-known Delta beauty, Martha Rose, who was no stranger to the Democratic Party in Tunica, the County seat of Tunica County. If truth be known, she had her sights set on one day becoming a Representative of the State of Mississippi. However, she had no knowledge of the events that could change her ambitions.

Lawrence and Liz's eldest son, Bill, had inherited his grandmother Martha Rose's looks, as well as her charm. Bill had two other siblings, Mary Katherine, and Sarah Elizabeth. It probably depended on who you talked to, as to what conclusion you would come to respecting whether one or all of the Lawson children were spoiled. It seemed like everybody in the county had an opinion. You know opinions are like noses, everybody has one.

Bill, with his good looks and charm, had dazzled most of the girls in more than one County, and they wanted to date him in the worst way. However, with that being said, he always kept his wits about him and never let it go to his head.

Mary Katherine, although named after her grandmother, Mary, unfortunately, had not inherited her beauty, and most definitely, not her charm. She was wild as a buck and determined to have things her way.

Sarah Elizabeth, being the baby of the three, was the apple of her daddy's eye. Although most folks believed she was aware of this fact, if she did, she never used it to her advantage. As a matter of fact, she would go out of her way to help anyone in need. It never hurt that her daddy had money but being rich was not the driving force behind Sarah.

It was Bill's twenty-first birthday; Lawrence and Liz had purchased him a brand-new black truck. For years, he had made it obvious that that was his heart's desire. Every time he was at the local Chevrolet dealership, he would not leave until he had looked over the trucks which had newly arrived. Up until this time, he had driven the old 1946 International farm truck and never complained.

They were planning on celebrating his birthday at the Blue & White Restaurant located just inside Tunica on Highway 61. They had invited a lot of Bill's friends.

They had gone to great lengths to keep the secret. If you did not watch out, Mary Katherine would intentionally spill the beans, just to ruin the surprise for her parents and brother. Thankfully, it appeared this time she had happiness abound rather than turmoil.

All the decorations, as many as would be acceptable to a twenty-one-year-old young man, had been arranged. A buffet had been set for all to choose from. It was made certain that catfish, hush puppies, and coleslaw were offered on the buffet, for these were Bill's favorite foods.

Randy Edwards, the owner of the Blue & White, had reserved the back room for the party and he had called Bill to stop by to check out his new black truck. He knew Bill would fall for the bait.

Everyone was in the back room waiting for the cue that Bill was coming inside. Randy saw Bill pull in behind the restaurant. He untied his apron, grabbed the keys and headed out the back door.

"Hi, there, Bill," he called out. "Wait until you see what I have parked in my parking spot."

"Howdy, sir, it is good to see you," he said. Both guys walked a short distance around the corner and there before them was this shiny black Chevy truck.

"Wow, what a beauty, sir. Do you mind if I sit in it?" "That's what I hoped you would ask."

"By all means," Randy told him as he handed him the keys. Bill opened the door and slid behind the steering wheel. The engine began to rumble as he turned the key.

"What a great sound and she's a total beauty," he said as he grinned at Mr. Edwards. Randy could not wait to ask him if he wanted to drive it.

The words just glided out of his mouth, "Would you like to take her out for a spin?" By this time Randy was grinning from ear to ear as he made the offer.

"Oh, gosh, sir, do you mean it?" Bill questioned.

"Please, Bill, call me Randy," was Randy's request.

"Yes, sir, Randy," he responded.

He carefully backed the truck out of the parking space and headed her out onto Highway 61.

"She drives great. I know you are so proud to own this beauty. I just can't say enough good stuff about her. It even has the gear shift on the floor. Sir, I mean, Randy, I pray God forgives me for my envy because I sure wish for one like her."

"You know I have waited a long time for this day to come. Anyway, Bill, I bet your dad will give you the keys to one before long. Don't you think so?" Randy asked, just about to burst inside. He was thinking all the while he had to keep his cool and not give the surprise away. "What about if you stay for some supper?" Randy threw out.

"You bet, sir, I mean Randy, I don't know if I will ever get used to calling you Randy," he said with a grin.

They drove back to the restaurant and Bill handed him the keys.

"Thank you, Randy, I appreciate you letting me drive her," he told him as they strolled toward the front door. Randy knew that the group could see him coming into the restaurant when he entered by way of the front door, so they would be ready for the surprise.

It was a Friday night and the restaurant was packed. "Why don't you and I go to the room in the back, where it is quiet, while we eat and talk? What is your choice of drink?" Randy asked.

"I'll take a Coke, please, sir," Bill said as he worked his way through the crowd.

"Howdy, Bill," one of his friends, Jeff, said in passing. Bill grinned and tipped his cowboy hat. He was dressed in black jeans, a western shirt, and wearing his cowboy boots. He had a fine-looking cowboy hat. It was deep caramel in color with quail feathers around the brim. Bill not only wore the clothes for looks, but he was quite the cowboy to boot. He could control the livestock with the best of them on his Quarter Horse, Cheyenne.

So far so good, thought Liz, as she felt her adrenaline rising. She could feel her hands sweating. Not only did they have to keep the party a surprise but keep the new truck a surprise. She could only hope that no one at the party would 'let the cat out of the bag."

"Quiet, everyone, Bill is just outside the door," Liz whispered. Only moments later the door opened and Bill stepped in. On cue, everyone jumped up and yelled "Surprise!" If Bill was not surprised, then he surely did a great job hiding it.

The first person who caught his eye was his mom. He could not help himself but head towards her.

"Mom, you pulled one over on me. This was totally a surprise," he said as he leaned in to give her a kiss on her forehead.

"Happy birthday, Son," she calmly said, squeezing his hand. She wondered if he felt her hands were wet from anticipation.

Lawrence rose to his feet and tapped his glass with a case knife. "All of you know it is our son's twenty-first birthday and we wish you," he said looking directly at Bill, "a very happy birthday. The buffet foods are all ready, so all of you get in line and enjoy all you can eat but remember, the birthday guy goes first." With that, Law strolled over and touched Bill on the shoulders and leaned in, once again, to wish him a happy birthday. "Go on over and help your plate, Son," and with that, Lawrence walked into the front to check how things had gone with Randy. He was assured that, to his knowledge, Bill was none the wiser.

A group of Bill's closest friends had pooled their money and purchased tickets to an up-and-coming singer, Johnny Cash, at an outdoor concert in Memphis, Tennessee. Johnny was a rockabilly singer and Bill loved his music. They had also arranged for Bill and a date to have dinner at the Blue Bayou in Clarksdale, Mississippi, a dinner theater owned by the Cook family.

While at the Blue Bayou they would enjoy entertainment from one of the Cook's sons, Sam, a new singer. Sam had a mellow voice that could captivate any audience. Although the artists had different musical styles in tempo, melody, and rhythm, etc. Bill enjoyed most of the up-and-coming musicians.

"I thank you all very much for these great gifts," Bill expressed as he took his seat.

Bill already had in mind the girl he would be asking if only Mr. Earl would let her go up to Memphis with him. It was Delta, but she certainly was unaware of it.

So far, Lawrence and Liz could not have asked for things to go any better. Lawrence rose to his feet and once again, tapped his glass and said, "Everyone, may I have your attention. We are so glad that you came to share in the celebration of Bill's birthday. We hope you have enjoyed your dinner. Now, everyone, drive safely home or wherever you might be going."

Of course, everyone was in on the planned surprise, which would occur outside the restaurant. They arranged it so Bill would be the last one to walk outside. During the time everyone was enjoying their meal, Liz gave two of Bill's buddies a big red bow, with the instructions to place it on the top of Bill's new truck. Randy quietly drove the truck directly under the lights from the door where the group would exit.

All the folks stood in two lines, creating a path from the restaurant door to the truck. Bill walked out the door. His eyes immediately locked on to the truck, but it seemed to take a minute for his brain to connect the dots. Then his mouth flew open as the words came flowing out.

"Dad, Mom, did you… Is this…" he said as he let out a cowboy yell and threw his hat in the air! After he strolled down the aisle, his dad handed him the keys to his brand-new truck. It was truly an unforgettable night!

***

Leroy, the rooster, gave out the early morning wake-up call. It took a second for Bill to wipe his eyes, sit up in bed, and truly realize that the night before had not been a dream. It was real. He dressed in his work clothes and walked down the stairs to get breakfast.

"Good morning, Son, I hope you slept well last night," Liz smiled as the words came from her mouth.

"You bet I did. You and Dad have made me the happiest guy in the world. I hope you know that," he said as he gave his mom a huge hug and immediately questioned, "Where is Dad?"

"He had to run to Clarksdale this morning. He is looking into buying a new combine," Liz informed him.

Bill ate his breakfast as quickly as he could, for he could

not wait to get to the barn, saddle up Cheyenne, and go for a ride.

"Mom, do you want to go for a ride with me? Now, I mean horseback, just to clarify."

"No, not today for me, I have to make a trip into Tunica and pick up a few things. But you enjoy your ride. I will see you for supper, for sure," she answered while walking toward the stairs. Immediately, Liz turned around and laughing out loud, she added, "Oh, by the way, enjoy your new truck."

"Cheyenne," Bill yells, simultaneously giving out a whistle that he has heard since he was a colt.

Cheyenne was sired by a stallion named Lone Wolf, and a mare named Silhouette. Although Bill understood that horses preferred to foal alone, he was of the opinion that Silhouette would feel better if he was nearby, so he made a comfortable bed of hay just on the other side of her stall.

It was a little past four in the morning of May 3, 1960, when Bill awakened with what he knew would be the birth. Keeping his distance, he watched as this beautiful foal was born. He could tell that Silhouette was going to be a good mother because immediately she began to create a bond with her new foal by licking and nuzzling it. Bill could see that Silhouette had given birth to a colt and he already had a name picked out, Cheyenne.

He could clearly understand why he would not be at the barn, for he was running far behind today.

Bill always knew that he had one of the fastest horses in the county, for Cheyenne had a strong, well-muscled body, broad chest and powerful, rounded hindquarters. He could run a short distance over a straightaway faster than any other horse he had run against. Cheyenne was a beautiful palomino and stood at sixteen hands high. When Bill mounted him, he stood tall in the saddle and was ready to challenge any other horse. He felt that this was a fact, not a brag.

It only took one more whistle and there came Cheyenne out from behind the only forested area on the farm.

"Come here, big guy," he called as he held out his hands to greet him; he gobbled up the half of the apple that was in his hand. He had total confidence in Bill. He nuzzled right under his arm.

"Let's go saddle up and get ready for a ride," Bill whispered into his ear. He followed straight behind him directly into the barn.

First, he brushed Cheyenne, carefully watching for any dirt or grit that needed to be removed. He brushed until the hair was lying flat. He was standing beside his neck, facing forward with the bridle in his left hand, and then he slipped the reins over Cheyenne's neck. He held the bridle up over his nose and with his right hand, using his left fingers, he held the bit against his mouth and slid the bit in. He grasped the crown of the bridle with his left hand and with his right hand he gently bent Cheyenne's right ear forward to slip it underneath the crown. After slipping the halter off, he smoothed the forelock, then he mounted him and they were off for a morning ride.

Chapter Three

The Spring Dance

Everybody that was anybody would be at the dance tonight. It was the social event of the spring. Delta and her best friend from school, Judy, were getting ready. Judy, you know the rule, we must look our best. Delta has chosen a deep purple dress that she knew flatters her shapely figure. Exactly how much makeup Daddy would let her walk out of the door wearing would be a touchy situation. So, she applied all that she felt made her look appealing, just not like a floozy. She knew Daddy would disapprove of that, and so did she.

Judy wore a stunning, radiant pink dress with a Queen Anne neckline and the prettiest necklace in the world. She was a strawberry blonde, blue-eyed beauty but she was beautiful inside too. They had been friends since the first grade, so they could almost complete each other's sentences. They stood face to face to take a good look at each other. If the guys did not take notice of us tonight, then they were blind, was pretty much their consensus.

The two girls entered the living room with all the confidence in the world. They figured this would be the best way not to draw any attention to the makeup that had been applied. It worked.

"Goodnight, Daddy and Mama. I will be home at the right

time," Delta said, pausing just long enough to let them know what to expect.

"Thank you, Mr. and Mrs. Daze, I had a wonderful visit," Judy complimented as the girls were coming closer to the door. Off they went for what they hoped would be a fun night.

They could see from the cars that most of the community folk were there. But the black truck that Delta was most interested in seeing appeared not to be there. Judy parked her car. They both made a quick inspection just to make certain everything was still in place, then they were off to make their entrance. The community center was just as they had suspected, packed. As they entered, they could feel that all eyes were on them.

"Wow," Judy whispered to Delta, "I did not expect this. How long do you think it will be before we will be asked to dance?"

As soon as the words were spoken, Bill walked up to Delta. He placed his hand just above the elbow and said, "You are dancing with me," without a question in his mind that she would say no.

Of course she would not. He looked so very handsome. He wore blue jeans with a black shirt and a camel-colored jacket. The way the black stood out next to the jacket was making Delta' as hot as a firecracker! She spoke not a word until they reached the dance floor. It was a slow dance. His cologne was intoxicating.

Bill was a great dancer. It was so easy to follow him. They were so spellbound with each other. As they glided across the floor, they had not noticed that everyone gave way just to watch them move so gracefully to the music.

Delta thought of all those times Daddy taught her how to

dance. He always emphasized that she should always let the man lead. On this night, while being held in Bill's arms, his leading was not a problem at all.

"You are quite the dancer. Someone has taught you well," Bill complimented.

She did not believe that it was the basics that Daddy had taught her. "Thank you, and so are you," She replied. Then she queried, "I did not see your truck when we arrived?"

"I always park it in the back of the building. Mr. Spencer, the manager of the community center, doesn't mind. I do not want a scratch on it. I believe it would push me to put a bullet in someone," Bill said, as he combed through his beautiful black hair.

Delta wanted to reach out and touch it. She watched as every black hair just fell into place.

He scarcely left her side for the entire evening, for that she was not complaining. This evening had already been far more than she had imagined. The only thing lingering in her mind was what in the world Daddy and Mama would say. After all, this was Bill Lawson. Also, she wondered if he could possibly feel what she was feeling for him. Delta believed that it had always been love at first sight for her.

"Delta," then there was a slight hesitation, "do you think it would be all right if I take you home?" he awkwardly choked out.

"If you promise not to drive too fast," knowing all along that he would not have to promise her anything.

All of the kids in the area simply loved his truck. He always made sure that it was sparkling clean. It had a stick shift on the floor and when he changed gears from second to third, his hand touched Delta's knee. She tried her best to make sure she was positioned where it would, for it sent shivers up her spine.

"Delta, did I tell you how pretty you look tonight," he stated in a bashful manner.

She did not believe there could be a bashful bone in his body. He could not help but know that most, if not all of the girls, wished they were in her shoes right now, but it was not for her to question. He had just paid her a wonderful compliment. I wonder if he knows that I am only sixteen, she questioned to herself almost forgetting to give him a thank you.

"Thank you. I am glad you think so. You look quite handsome yourself, just in case I have not told you." To her, he was absolutely movie-star handsome.

"Do you mind if we make a stop at the reservoir dam?" he hesitantly asked.

She knew this was the parking spot for teens in the area but somehow, she knew that he would be a gentleman and not let things get out of hand.

"No, just as long as I get home on time."

Bill's kisses were intoxicating. Their bodies pulsated as he pulled her closer. She gently caressed his skin and could feel his heart beating with excitement. Tenderly, they embraced. His erotic touch pleaded to be satisfied. Bill pulled back momentarily to gaze into Delta's eyes. It seemed like a moment and an eternity all at the same time. It seemed as if he could see inside her soul.

His lips met hers affectionately. It was a passionate kiss, one Delta would never forget. It was all she could do to restrain her desire to have him touch her in places pulsating to be satisfied, in ways only a man could do. His silky hair slid through her fingers as her hands reached his muscular chest. She could feel his heart beating with a burning yearning to be completed with sensuous intercourse.

"Make love to me, Delta," Bill whispered. Feeling his muscular chest next to her breast, she wanted to give in with every fiber of her being, but she knew she could not.

"Bill, I can't. It is not that I don't want to. I could let it happen so easily, but not now."

He pulled back, looking at her, desiring to understand, for he knew she felt as he did. Tears rolled down her cheek and she wiped them away.

"I love you," rolled out of her mouth before she could even stop it. "Oh, I think you know that," she whispered. "But you know how I have been raised. I know how disappointing it would be for Daddy and Mama, not to mention God, should things turn out wrong." She believed he understood exactly what she was trying to explain.

Delta watched him as he was trying to digest this. She wondered how many girls had been at these crossroads and given in to their desires.

Gently he slid his hands down around her waist. Deep inside him was a feeling of love for her too, but he could not, at this moment, bring that truth to the surface.

Moments passed and he placed a kiss on her cheek. She knew she was safe with him. Why other people could not see this side of him was beyond her.

"I had better get you home. You know how your daddy can be if we are not there pretty close to his time," Bill stated with a sheepish grin.

The bright moonlit sky made Delta wish this night did not have to end. She reached over and ran her fingers through his hair one more time. She loved how that made her feel and with all her heart she knew that someday she would be able to give her complete self to Bill.

A gentle breeze was blowing as they reached the front porch. He pulled her close to him as if to say, it's all right. He gazed into her eyes and then gave her a goodnight kiss. She stood just inside the door, watching as he pulled out of the driveway, heading for home. The evening had been perfect. Walking inside she wondered what she would say to Daddy in the morning when he asked her how she got home. She never wanted to lie to him so she hoped that when she said Bill Lawson, he would somehow understand.

At breakfast the next morning nothing was said about the Spring Dance, and Delta liked that just fine.

"What field are you going to be working in today, Daddy?" Delta asked, planning all along to drop by with a sausage biscuit in the hopes he would let her drive the tractor a row or two. She loved that old green John Deere tractor because she knew how pleased it made her Daddy when she took an interest in the things he did; she lived to please her daddy.

"Oh, I guess I had better work down in the New Ground," Daddy said as he picked up his cap, rubbed back his gray hair, and put it on. He went out the back door.

"Mama, do you care if I take Daddy another sausage biscuit later?" Delta asked with the sincere belief that Mama would not mind.

"Delta, I have quite a few chores that need doing around here; I don't need you running off piddling off half of the day somewhere in those fields," Mama spat back.

From the tone in Mama's voice, Delta knew it would be

better to let this one pass. There would be other times to drive the tractor; Mama worked hard and she was sure that she could use the help, although it was not what she had in mind for the day.

Delta loved her mama and wanted to please her but it was her daddy that hung the moon and the stars. She would do anything to do the very best job for him but with Mama, quality work was not always on her mind. Mama was no pushover, for she would always come in to inspect the work Delta had just declared she had finished.

"Delta, are you telling me that this room has been thoroughly swept?" Mama would question.

"Yep," would usually be Delta's reply, just hoping for a passing grade.

"Just look over here in this corner. Do you call that clean? Get the broom, missy, and start all over. The next time I come in here, this room had better be clean," Mama demanded before turning to leave the room.

Delta could not help it, for it made her so mad. She would never let Mama see her, but as she turned to leave the room, she immediately stuck her tongue out at her.

This was usually how most of the chores went as each was completed. Either Delta's heart was just not in pleasing Mama or, in her opinion, Mama just expected too much.

Finally, the day was over. Delta could relax a while and do a little dreaming about Bill. Would he be driving somewhere in his truck, she wondered. She tried to imagine that tan body from the top of his head to the bottom of his feet, with anything in-between. What in the world would Daddy think of 'his baby girl', thinking these kinds of thoughts? Probably, he would be pretty displeased but what Daddy didn't know would not hurt him, so the saying goes, that was fine with Delta.

"Delta, get in here and set the table. You know your daddy will be driving up any time now and he will be ready for supper," Mama spoke loudly from the kitchen.

Oh, Mama, just leave it to you to interrupt all these wonderful thoughts. She should be calling Peggy, Delta thought. With Mama, it seemed that Peggy could get away with murder, but she pulled her body up from the bed and headed to the kitchen, being certain not to let Mama see her displeasure. Anyway, Daddy would be home soon and for that she was glad.

Supper went as it usually did until Daddy asked Delta a question. Breaking a piece of bread and dipping it in the bacon gravy, he took a big bite and spoke, "Delta, what do you say about going into town with me tomorrow?"

"Oh, Daddy, I would like to go. "Why are we going?", Delta asked quickly.

Now that question is stupid, she thought. I want to go no matter the reason, for Delta knew that going into town always meant the chance of running into Bill. This was because Bill and Daddy were always working on a project together. For a few minutes, she laid there with great anticipation of the events which might happen the next day.

Chapter Four

Queen for a Day!

Daddy did not have to tell Delta twice to get out of bed. "I'll be ready in a minute, Daddy," Delta spoke, wanting him to know how very excited she was to be going with him.

"You take time to eat some breakfast, Delta, for we will be in town for quite a while today," Daddy told her, patting her on the head as he passed by.

This was an exciting day for him as well but Delta had no idea of what was in store for her. She just wanted a chance to see Bill. She ate the oatmeal with a biscuit and drank down a large glass of milk.

"There, Daddy, that should hold me," Delta said as she rushed over to give Mama a kiss goodbye.

Daddy drove a 1948 blue Chevrolet truck with the shift on the floor. Delta absolutely loved this truck. This was the truck she drove when she got her driver's license.

"You get behind the wheel, Delta," Daddy instructed. Delta would not argue that driving this truck was like steering a new truck. She pushed the clutch with her left foot, placed the stick shift into reverse and backed up; then, she put the shift into first gear and they were off. Off for exactly what was still a mystery to Delta but any time spent with Daddy was a treat.

"Delta," Daddy said, "I want you to drive over to Leon Alderson's house because I need to borrow something."

Pulling the truck into the driveway, Delta and Daddy got out and walked to the door where Leon was already waiting for them.

"Good morning, Earl and Delta," Leon greeted them with a warm welcome. Can I get you anything to drink or eat?" he offered as they walked through the door."

"No thank you, Leon, we have had a big breakfast and have a long day ahead of us so I think it is best we make our visit short," was Daddy's reply.

Delta was still wondering what was going to take so long.

Leon closed the back door behind us and we headed toward the barn.

"Earl, I have the trailer all cleaned out for you. It should be in good shape; you should not have any problems," Leon spoke with confidence.

"Delta, go back the truck up so we can hitch it to this trailer," Daddy told Delta. She never questioned Daddy but did just as she was told.

They pulled away from the barn. Daddy gave Leon a big wave goodbye and a big holler that he would see him later.

The dust billowed from behind the big white trailer. Delta had never driven a truck with something attached to it but she drove it like a pro. She glanced over at Daddy and could not help but wonder, what in the world was he up to? What did this day hold? Due to all of the events, she had not given Bill much of a thought.

"You think you can handle everything when you reach the highway," Daddy questioned Delta, "or do you want me to take over from here?"

"Not at all, Daddy, I can handle it. I want to drive all the way into town," Delta confidently answered.

"We will be taking a left when we reach Clayton, then head out to Steven's ranch," Daddy told Delta. Now, this was really piquing Delta's interest.

They pulled up in front of the big white barn. Several of the cowhands walked over to greet us. "Mornin', Mr. Earl," one of them spoke up as he spat brown snuff out of his mouth. He was decked out in his 'cowboy' attire — chaps, cowboy boots, and plaid shirt, etc. He seemed as if he knew what he was doing.

"I have several horses that Mr. Stevens told me to round up that you might be interested in purchasing," the young man told Daddy.

Purchasing, I thought as I crossed my eyes over to Daddy. I knew that he could read the confusion on my face. Oh, my, this could not be true, but maybe, just maybe it was. I have always wanted a horse. I pinched myself. I was not dreaming.

Daddy was looking directly at me as he began his cautionary discourse, "Delta, these young men are going to be bringing one of these horses for you to ride. Now, if at any time you feel uneasy and nervous about the handling of the horse, you just let them know and they will take the reins. Is that understood?" he asked with a serious voice.

"Daddy, what in the world is happening? Am I, I mean, are you serious? Are one of these horses going to be mine?" I questioned with a little reluctance from not believing it was really true.

"You bet it is. However, I want you to be certain that you can handle the horse and that it is the one for you. Is that clear, Delta?" he spoke with sternness in his voice.

The guy, Gus, who greeted us at the beginning, brought the first horse from out of the huge barn. I wondered how many horses were there. Gus held the reins as I mounted the beautiful bay mare.

"Are you comfortable, Miss Delta?" Gus questioned.

I was not sure if I was or not but I knew I wanted a horse more than words could possibly say. Also, I wanted to be sure that it was the right one.

"I'm okay," I said as he handed me the reins.

"Just ride her out that way," he said, as he pointed toward the south, "then bring her back this way; now, you can ride her as long as you would like," he added.

The bay mare rode like a trained horse should ride. She was easy in the saddle, as Daddy would put it. I believe I fell in love with her from the get-go but there were more horses to ride before I made up my mind. I rode them all in the same pattern and many of them were nice horses, but they just could not compare with the bay mare. I knew in my heart she was the one I wanted.

"Delta, I believe these guys have given you a pretty good many horses to select from," Daddy said, looking directly into my eyes. "What will it be, Delta?"

My heart was pounding out of my chest and I still wondered if I was dreaming.

"Daddy, I want the first horse, the bay mare," I said with conviction.

"Bring her around, guys, so we can load her into the trailer," Daddy said as he took his cap off to wipe the sweat from his forehead.

As I stood there looking at him, my heart was as full of love as it could possibly be. I wanted that moment in time to freeze so I could preserve it. I ran toward him and threw my arms around his slender body, hugging him with all that was in me.

"Thank you, thank you, Daddy. I love you so very much," I said with tears rolling out of my eyes. As he hugged me back, I noticed several tears rolling out of his eyes.

One of the cowhands, Keith, kept looking at me. It made me feel slightly uneasy. Maybe this was because I was not accustomed to 'this kind of look', then I noticed he was walking toward me. He took his hat off. He was a nice-looking young man, but there always seemed like there was only one guy I thought about, and that was Bill. However, I was young and who knew where it was going with Bill. I was always aware of how popular Bill was with the girls.

"Miss Delta, you did some fine riding out there," he spoke with a kind voice, "and I was wondering, if it is okay with Mr. Earl, I would like to call you sometime?" Keith said.

I turned to see where exactly Daddy had ventured off to and I saw him next to the back of the trailer.

"Thank you, maybe it is best if we go see Daddy," I said, all the while walking to where Daddy was standing.

As we reached the trailer, Keith reached out to shake Daddy's hand to introduce himself, "Hi, Mr. Earl, my name is Keith Stone. You might know my daddy, Bobby Gene Stone. We live just outside Independence."

"You bet I do know old Bobby Gene. He is a fine fellow," Daddy said as he shook Keith's hand.

"Sir, I just told your daughter what a fine job she did handling those horses. She rode like she has been around horses all her life," he spoke looking directly at my Daddy. I could feel my cheeks begin to blush. This kind of thing was totally new to me but I liked it!

"Sir," Keith continued on, not really giving Daddy much time to interject, "with your permission, sir, I would like to call Delta. Would that be all right with you?"

I looked at Daddy and he was looking directly at Keith. I was uncertain what was going to come out of his mouth.

"Keith, I tell you what, I will give you the directions to our farm and if it is pleasing to Delta, you can come by for a Sunday dinner; nevertheless, first I have to run past my wife. You know how it is. It is okay with me, if Delta wants, to give you our phone number but there will be no date until a later time. Is that understood?" Daddy spoke while, again, shaking his hand.

"Yes, sir, I understand. I appreciate it, thank you, sir," Keith joyfully spoke the words and turned to me. Oh, my, I thought, what do I do now?

He reached for a piece of paper from out of his blue jeans. It seemed as if he was prepared for this moment in time.

"Please, Delta, may it be as your Daddy spoke? Will you allow me to give you a call?" he questioned.

The piece of paper felt slightly damp because it was hot outside; he had been working. I wrote our telephone number then handed the paper back to him.

"It has been nice to meet you and I hope to hear from you," I said as I turned to walk back to the truck. I could tell Keith was watching me as I walked off. This was the first time that I was aware of a guy seeing me like a lady. Honestly, I liked it!

I opened the passenger door and as Daddy got on the other side, he questioned if I still wanted to drive, since there was something in the trailer, meaning it might be a challenge. I looked at him as if to say, are you kidding me, I am going to let these guys think I can't handle this? He knew without a word being spoken exactly what was coming from my eyes.

"Well," Daddy said after pulling away from the Steven's Ranch, or The Circle S Ranch it was known by, "it looks like you got more than a horse from this deal?"

"Oh, Daddy," I said with my face blushing as I reached over and slapped his knee. The cab of that truck was so full of love on that late spring afternoon.

"Delta, I have planned on one more stop, but you can't take all day in making up your mind because we have special cargo in that trailer to think about. I want you to drive through Olive Branch to that boots store, for I want you to pick out a pair of boots and a cowgirl hat," he spoke as he directed me to take a right turn onto Highway 78.

"Daddy, that is just too much. You buying me the horse is plenty," I said with deep sincerity.

"Now, Delta, I can't have you riding that beautiful mare without being all decked out yourself. Now, that just cannot be," he stated with clarity.

I parked the truck and trailer at the side of the small store but to my surprise, upon entering the store, there was more western stuff than a person could imagine. But it did not take me long before I was at the counter with boots, spurs and a cowgirl hat, ready to checkout.

From the time I got out of bed, I could not have possibly imagined what this day held for me. It was a girl's dream come true.

"Daddy, I hope you know how very much I love you, but not just because of all you have done for me," I spoke while holding his big strong hand, worn from the hard work he did.

"I love you too, Delta," he said shyly as he quickly changed the subject. "Now, what are you going to name that bay mare we have back there?" he questioned.

Without hesitation, I said, "Queen."

Chapter Five

The Rape

"Wake up, kids. We need to talk to you," Daddy' spoke in a different tone.

I wiped the sleep from my eyes and eased out of bed. Peggy was never one to react to Daddy's first request but I knew this should not be one of those days. I poked her in her side.

"Quit," she snarled back.

"Peggy, something is going on and I don't think this is the day to push Daddy's patience," I spoke back and turned her over so that I could see her face.

We both arrived in the kitchen where Mama and Daddy were already drinking their coffee.

"The oats are on the stove. You girls go ahead and help yourself to plates," Mama spoke, wanting our bellies to be full for whatever was coming.

Daddy started the conversation off, "Looks like Mavis is going to have her baby today. I know that I am going to take your Mama up there to be with her. I am going to leave it up to you if you go or stay but should you decide to stay here, you had better remember the rules."

Peggy quickly chimed in that she wanted to be there. I, on the other hand, did not like to be around sickness of any kind, even having a baby. I would rather see the baby at another time.

"Daddy, even though Peggy is going, will you please let me stay here?" I questioned, believing the idea would not be received well.

"Delta, anything can happen, you know that. You being here by yourself just gives me an uneasy feeling," Daddy said, trying to reason with me.

"Please, oh, please. I have some homework that I need to do; I promise I will stay close to home." Mama had already left to get things ready but now reappeared in the kitchen.

"Pesh," he used Mama's nickname, "Peggy wants to go but Delta is asking to stay here. What do you think we should do?" Daddy asked, probably hoping she would say no.

But to all our surprise, Mama guessed it would be okay.

I could still tell that Daddy had some serious reservations because they would be driving all the way to Horn Lake, about thirty-five miles away, but he finally agreed.

I watched as the pickup sped up the road. Speed means about thirty-five miles an hour. Okay, what should I do first, I asked myself? I knew all the cows would have been milked, the hens' eggs gathered, but there were likely some vegetables that needed picking.

First, I turned on the record player and danced in the living room. I felt so happy. I got to have the day to myself. I felt grown up and very much alive! Okay, that's enough; I wanted to do something that would please Mama and Daddy and show them how responsible I am.

I put on my bonnet and went out the back door. Sure enough, there were tomatoes, okra, and peas that needed attention. All the while, I was thinking about how proud Daddy

44

will be of me for picking the vegetables.

I had my buckets full and, to be honest, I was exhausted. We had a small room just off the porch where we cleaned up from having worked outside. I drew some water in the small washbasin and while taking a washcloth, I washed myself off. It made me feel so fresh. I put on a clean dress and walked into the kitchen.

After grabbing a biscuit from off the stove, I turned around and Jerry Bennett was standing directly in front of me with two guys, one on each side of him.

"How in the world did you guys get in here?" my voice questioned, demanding an answer. "Look, Daddy & Mama are out at the barn and should be back soon for lunch," I hastily said, hoping that they would believe me.

"You lying sack of shit. Your Daddy and Mammy are nowhere around here. We saw them in Dubbs with that fine-looking sister of yours. Looked to me like they were headed on a trip, not to no fucking barn. So, why don't you just cut the crap and let us get down to business," were the words that came out of the lying creep, Jerry's mouth.

"Now we have this all planned out so don't do anything dumb or you will regret it, we promise. We want this to go according to our plans. We don't really care for any of your ideas. You got it?" were the words coming from his mouth as brown snuff dripped from the corners. He pulled his left arm up and wiped it on his shirt sleeve.

"Who else is here?" I asked, trying to divert his attention. It wasn't working.

"Bitch, quit asking questions. We are here and that is all you need to know, so shut your fucking mouth," he shouted as one of the other guys shoved me down onto the couch.

Thoughts were racing through my head about how many times I have been warned about this guy. He's no stranger, but he may as well be. Don't ever find yourself along with any of the Bennett boys, especially that Jerry, Mama would warn. I got it, but this situation was beyond my control. I had no idea he was anywhere around the vicinity; but here he was in our house, certainly on no invitation of mine. Now, here are two other deranged guys with who knows what on their minds.

"Money, Jerry, I will try and find you some money," I pleaded. I was so nervous. Please God don't let this happen, knowing Jerry did not care whether God approved of this or not.

"Anyone here or coming?" he questioned.

"I'm unsure," I whispered. Wrong answer, I thought. Trying to correct the wrong I said, "The family will not be gone for long." I could tell that he did not believe this.

"We're going to do this thing," Jerry said as he tore a sleeve off my dress. I tried to think of a way out of this situation; I could not see it. If only someone would drive up — anybody.

He pulled my dress up and pulled off my panties. His hands felt so coarse and even his smell was making me sick to my stomach. None of the Bennett boys were bad looking, they were just crude and downright mean.

How could this possibly be happening? I was saving myself for someone special, hopefully, Bill, but now I will be forever tarnished. There was no tenderness; there could be nothing tender about this brutal, sinful attack.

I was afraid to say anything about the fact that Daddy would track him down like a dog and kill him on the spot, for I feared he would kill me there on the spot. I had not seen any weapon but there could be one anywhere.

"Jerry, please, every damn one of you just leave. Don't do this," I uttered through my tears.

"Shut the hell up. This is going to happen, bitch," he uttered. After these words, there came a slap across my face. It made my cheek burn. This is an animal, I thought. "Anyway, after I am finished, I know Wayne is waiting to get some of this good stuff. That is all I have heard the son-of-a-bitch talk about for about a week," Jerry was quick to inform.

Oh, how I wished Mavis would not have gone into labor on this day. I wished Peggy had not gone to Mavis'. Someone, please come home! Time is running out for me.

He spread my legs and began to push inside me. It hurt so badly. I was a virgin. I screamed out in pain. I felt like I would split in two. I could feel the blood on the sofa cover underneath me. Then I realized that it, too, was part of his fluids. I wanted to throw up. I felt so ashamed and totally mortified.

He lay back on the sofa from exhaustion. I looked at him. I don't believe I ever hated anyone before but I totally hated this degenerate.

It seems like no time after Jerry pulled out, this guy, Wayne, was pulling me toward him, and he began the same process, dirty hands and all. This guy was even rougher. He tears the top of my dress off, and begins fondling my breasts and licking my nipples. Oddly enough, I could feel my nipples were sensitive to the touch. I felt confused. How can this be? I did not want to feel anything, certainly not in a good way, were my thoughts while he was doing these horrifying things. He was a very muscular man; there was no way I could fight him off. Oh, God, please help me.

"Please, don't, please don't, my body will not be able to

take it," I begged. I wept.

"Shut up," he said as he caught me by the hair. "Tease me," he demanded, "You just don't know how long I have waited for this day."

"You have been planning this?" I said with shock.

I wanted him to stop. "Stop," I screamed, but it did not seem to faze him. He just kept pushing harder and deeper inside me.

Finally, he reached his climax and lay in what seemed to me as exhaustion and ecstasy in one. This was too new for me to know what exactly was happening. The one thing I did know is that I hated it.

"Please, I am going to be sick. You have done what you came to do, so leave before Daddy gets home. I will not say a word about what has happened here. Please leave," was my desperate plea.

"Oh no, little lady," Jerry grinned as he spoke, "There is one more guy, possibly more anxious than Wayne to get his share. So, just buckle up buttercup; you are still in for the time of your life because from what I have been told, old Max is hung like a mule." All these horrible words were spilling from this disgusting guy's mouth, one that I wanted to slap so hard but I knew could spell death. I did not understand everything they were talking about because all of it sounded savage to me.

This guy that they called Max was the cruelest. He ripped all shreds of the clothing from my body. He began to bite me in places that, until now, I have only touched. His bites were hurting my breasts. "Please, stop doing that," I protested. But that only seemed to make him only more brutal. When he plunged his large manhood inside me, I thought that I would surely split in two. I held on to any part of the couch to try to ease the pain but little pain was being eased. Finally, he was finished with his cruel treatment of me. I rolled slightly onto my side, only to notice two legs standing in front of me. It was Jerry.

"Bitch, I am as horny as hell. I need some more of your wet kitty cat, but this time I will be last. There will be Wayne, Max, and then me. I want you to remember me," he said with a wild glare in his eyes.

These dreadful men did not care what harm that they were inflicting on me. Actually, I would be blessed to come out of this alive.

These actions took place until each man had raped me twice with Jerry being the last as he planned. I was so very afraid that it would happen a third time.

Jerry left and went into the kitchen. He found the pitcher of tea and fixed himself a glass.

"Would you like some tea," he asked me. What a son-of-a-bitch you are, I thought, but I said nothing.

He peaked around the corner from the kitchen. I thought to myself, this is some kind of a game for all of them and they are enjoying it. Should I run?

I ran for the door but he snatched me back. The sofa was wet but he pushed me back on it. I felt absolutely helpless. I wanted to scream but who would hear me? —No one.

"Why wouldn't I, you are beautiful and I knew it would be some good stuff. Look, one more time and we will go; just act like you are enjoying it," he says.

I thought to myself, I would have to be the greatest actress in the world to play that part, but I said nothing for anyone that could be this cruel could be a murderer too.

This time, he produces a knife. I guess he had gotten it

from the kitchen or brought it with him, I could not be sure. "Say you like it," he demanded.

"Okay, okay, I like it, just get this over with," I exhaustedly whispered. There was no use trying to reason with a crazy man. This time his ejaculation came quickly. I felt relieved. Maybe this terror will soon be over.

"You know exactly who we are so if you tell anyone we will return to kill all of you, do you understand," he shouted.

I was confused. Were they finally leaving after all of this terror? "I promise, I promise, no one will ever know. I would not want them to know. Just go," I begged.

"You know I could not say anything to Daddy. One, I would be too ashamed. Two, I am afraid of what will happen," I spoke hoping they would buy it.

I heard the door slam. They were gone. I ran to double lock the doors and closed all of the windows. I could see them walking across the field. Oh, thank God they are gone, I thought.

I gathered all of my clothes from the room. I would burn them at the first opportunity. I pulled the cover off the sofa. I had no idea how I would explain that to Mama. I had no way of washing any of it; all I could do would be to hide it. I boiled some water to fill the washtub and scrubbed every inch of my body; even then, I felt so dirty. My skin was reddening from my scrubbing. I just could not seem to get clean.

Daddy, and at least Peggy, will be home soon. I was running around trying to make sure everything was back in place. I wanted no evidence that anybody had been there.

I went to the back porch room and dressed in the clothes I had on earlier. They were sweaty but that was even better. I will act like I just came from the garden. I looked down and there were drops of blood on the floor. Oh, no, not this. I found one of Daddy's old t-shirts, tore it, and placed it in my panty crotch. I fell to my knees in tears. It was as if I had drifted into another world, so very foreign to me. No one must know of this. I would have to be a great actress to pull this off.

Then my mind rushed back to those very thoughts that had run through my brain hours before. He wanted me to be an actress, now I had to be one. I stood up slowly and went into the bedroom. Honestly, I wanted to hide but there was nowhere to go. This was the test of a lifetime. I wept and wept. I screamed but no one was there to hear.

I guess exhaustion put me to sleep but upon waking, I could hear the sound of Daddy, Mama, and Peggy getting out of the truck. I ran to the mirror. My eyes were red from crying. Just at that moment, Peggy entered the room.

"What is wrong with you?" she questioned.

"I went to the garden to gather the vegetables, a wasp stung me and it hurts," I said hoping for her to drop the issue.

"The wasp stung you where? Delta, move your hand so I can see. Come on, Peggy insisted. Let Daddy put some stuff on it."

"Let go, Sister, Don't worry about it. I have taken care of it. Anyway, I want to hear all about the new baby," I said to divert the attention away from me. It worked.

We both headed into the living room where Daddy and Mama were. Mavis had another boy and they named him James Earl; both the baby and Mavis were doing well.

Fortunately for me, this was the talk of the night. However, my mind was nowhere near that room. Right now, all that room held for me was the dreadfulness that had taken place earlier.

Mama spoke up, "Where is the sofa cover, Delta?"

So began my lies. "I spilled chocolate on it, so I pulled it off. I will wash it in the morning, if that is okay, Mama," speaking lies that were not part of my character. She seemed to believe it. There should not be anything out of place, except what they could not see — my crushed spirit, my lost virginity, and the fear building inside of me. I never even thought of the vegetables I had harvested with the great desire of how proud Daddy would have been.

It was early, but I had to get away. "Ya'll, I am going to bed," I said.

"Delta, are you sick?" were the immediate words out of Mama's mouth. Mama knew her children and she was picking up on something. Please do not pick up on this, not ever, I thought.

"No, Mama, I am just tired." All the while, I wanted to run to her for comfort. "This has been a long day. I will see everyone in the morning," I said to Mama while holding back the tears.

I wished so badly to seek the love and care of my Daddy but I could never hide something like this from him, not for one moment. If nothing else, he would see it in my eyes.

That night I held the quilt so close to my face I could hardly breathe. I was doing everything I could to muffle the sound of my sobbing from the family. How could I ever look at people the same? Oh, dear Jesus, how can I ever look into Bill's eyes knowing this dreadful thing has happened to me? How could I possibly live with this? Life was forever changed for me and I knew it.

The sun rose from the sky as it had always done. I felt like I wanted to die. Death could certainly have some comfort, couldn't it? Could I live through each and every day?

I could hear Daddy calling me to breakfast. I did not want a thing to eat. My stomach was churning now. I know it was nerves— but how do you stop your nerves, was my thought. It seemed to take forever to get to the kitchen. I just knew instantly that they were going to call me out on how I looked, and they did.

Mama immediately said, "Why, Delta, you look like something the cat would drag in. Are you sick?"

"Well, Mama, I guess I am. Can I go back to bed? I feel like I am sick to my stomach." I was speaking the truth. Mama pulled my head over to her shoulder. I know that she was trying to see if I had a fever, for once I hoped that I did.

"You go get back under the covers. I will come in a little later to check on you," she said all the while taking the biscuits to the table. Not even Mama's delicious biscuits smelled good to me.

After I entered my room, I reached for my hairbrush to brush through my hair but quickly abandoned that. I didn't care what I looked like. Oh, my, I pulled back my top only to see black and blue marks all over. How would I keep Mama from this examination? My mind was spinning ninety miles an hour. I had no answers. I had better get out of the house was all I could come up with, for if Mama enters that room, the jig will be up, there was no doubt about it.

I hurriedly put on the clothes that I had on yesterday. I did not care. I only wanted to be gone. Fortunately for me, everyone was too busy or in their own little world to even notice I left. I just began to drive and drive. I had no destination. Where could I go for help with this? I could not go to Bill or Keith. Who, who was my question? I drove to

Arkabulta Lake. It was pretty there. I threw rocks into the lake just to pass the time. I wondered if I would drown, like Daddy so many times warned. I did not want to drown. And then, I thought of the Catholic Father who was at Senatobia. I thought the world of him. He was such a smart man. Visiting him was my best option and, for the moment, my mind seemed eased.

A lady greeted me as I walked into the church. "May I help you, child?" she asked.

I shyly asked, "Is Father Ashberry here?"

She left the room. After a few minutes passed, she returned to lead me back to see Father Ashberry.

I was surprised to be meeting with him face to face and not in a confessional. Father Ashberry gave a polite smile and inquired how he could be of help? I could feel the tears as they rolled down my face but; somehow, I guess with God's help, I spoke the words, "I have been raped by three men."

The Father did not look shocked but how could he not be? How often does this kind of thing happen? The Father requested that we bow our heads in prayer. I did not hesitate for I knew that I needed God's help. He counseled me for about an hour and asked if I could return for twice-weekly sessions. Again, I agreed without hesitation for I knew how badly that I needed his counsel. I left feeling somewhat better but there still were so many lingering questions.

I had no idea that I would be plagued with nightmares. They seem to occur every night. Of course, it would keep me from sleeping. Some nights I would slip out into the barn just to talk to Queen. I knew she would tell no one. So, with Father Ashberry and Queen's help, my burden was lighter.

Somehow, I managed to keep this dreadful experience from the family. My black and blue bruises healed without anyone noticing; of course, that took creative planning on my part.

I did not ever want Daddy to see these scars but my spirit and mind were permanently scarred. They would be with me for the rest of my days.

Chapter Six

Life Changes for Delta

It had been only three days since the encounter with Jerry and 'the goons'. Delta had scarcely left the house. She knew she was becoming more and more withdrawn, and she hated the feeling. There seemed to be a dark hole in her heart and she had no idea how to repair it.

She knew Mama suspected something but never this. She had managed to find an opportunity to dispose of the ripped and stained clothes. Her plan was to burn them but due to all of the rainy days, her plan had changed. She went to a field on Mr. Mayo's property and buried them. She worked as hard as she could to get the blood and semen stains off the sofa cover and guessed it was unnoticeable, for Mama had not complained.

She felt so different inside. Her innocence had been taken. She hated herself. Even how she acted or reacted around the most special man in her life, her daddy, was different. She was in a horrifying place from which there was no escape.

Thank goodness there were only two more weeks of school left. She knew she would run into Jerry Bennett on the bus. He, too, was a senior this year. It was going to take everything in her not to react. Fortunately, Delta had only one class, English, with him, and he sat at the back of the class.

It had been two weeks since the rape. So far, Jerry had missed six out of ten days from school. The days he was there, she never made eye contact with him. The one time that she caught him out of her peripheral vision, he had a smug grin on his face. She immediately engaged in conversation with Judy, trying her best to ignore this creep.

Graduation day had come. She was very happy. She was out of school. She had not been feeling too well the past couple of weeks; maybe it was a stomach virus nagging her or just nerves from the graduation events. Both of these, she considered, could be causing it.

As badly as she hated it, she had intentionally avoided Bill and Keith. She had not even invited them to her graduation. They had to be wondering what was going on with her. Did she not love either of them any longer? That could never be the case; her heart was made to love Bill, for sure. She missed him so deeply but she just could not face him. She knew she would break down. This, pretending like everything was fine to her family, took all of the energy she had.

School is only out a few days before it is time to begin hoeing cotton. This year was going to be really hard because it would only be Daddy, Mama, and Delta to hoe all of the fields; all of these totaled about ten acres. In the rest of the land, Daddy planted soybeans — thank goodness, those only had to be plowed.

This year, due to illness, Thomas couldn't help out, nor Marshall because he had moved to Greenville, MS, to be closer to his family.

Daddy always tried to be certain that the cotton crop was 'laid by' (meaning it no longer could be hoed because the blooms on the cotton plants could be knocked off). These blooms were what produced cotton, so no blooms and no cotton equaled less money for the family to live on during the following year.

Thank goodness this year was no different to any other, on July 4th, the cotton crop was laid by. Soon, Delta would be taking her summer trip to visit Barbara. She always looked forward to that.

She had been working for Mr. Mayo hoeing cotton on the days that Daddy did not need her. As it turned out this season, she was able to work hoeing cotton for Mr. Mayo on the days that daddy didn't need her. Delta earned eighteen dollars, which gave her money to buy whatever she wanted.

Daddy never asked for the money Delta made on her own. He was always so very proud of her for she was always dependable to work on the family farm. It seemed like there was not a chore she could not, or would not, try to do.

Delta was sick and really missing Bill. Her appetite was not the same. It seemed like food just did not appeal to her, but all the same, she was gaining weight. Her clothes were fitting her tighter around the waist.

"Mama, I am so excited about next week. I will be spending it with Barbara." This seemed like the first time in weeks that Delta appeared happy.

"Barbara and I are planning on going to a movie theater to see *The Graduate*. Mama, Anne Bancroft is in it and there is a new actor, Dustin Hoffman, starring in it. You know what, Mama, Agnes is going to let us take the bus all the way to downtown Memphis! I have never ridden on a bus like that," she said.

Mama was taking it all in for it was the first time in weeks that she was seeing some of the Delta she knew.

"Do you think that Peggy will let me use a few clothes if I promise to bring them back safe and sound?" Delta questioned. She hoped Mama would put in a word for her to Peggy.

"Just ask your sister for what you want and I am sure she will share with you. Anyway, why should you need any of her clothes when you have plenty of your own to pick from?" Mama asked.

"Mama, you are not getting where I am coming from. I will just ask her myself, so don't bother, okay," she said emphatically.

"Are you eating a bunch of sweets at the store or when you go off to stay overnight with your friends?" she questioned. Mama was still irritated about the clothes not fitting.

"Yea, Mama, that must be what is happening, for it makes sense to me, so just stop worrying about it. Now, let's just drop it, okay?" I said as I was leaving the room.

I was tired of hearing it! I cannot remember a time that I seemed so easily upset at Mama. I adored her. What is going on with me, I wondered. I knew Peggy would lend me the clothes, so why had I made it into such a big deal?

Agnes, Newton and the family were on their way down. This is the Sunday I will be going home with them. I wondered if Barbara was as excited as I was. I had everything packed. I made sure I had $18.00 in my purse. I was certain the week would be like none other; at least I will have a change of scenery, so maybe my nerves would ease up a bit.

Newton was always known for his fast driving. I watched the dust flying from behind the 1956 Buick as we drove down the gravel road headed toward Memphis. I was so glad to just get away.

"Newton, you need to slow down on these roads," Agnes pleaded, but it appeared to fall on deaf ears, for he kept rolling on.

The car pulled onto Verne Road, only a few houses away from 102 Verne. I had written that number so many times in my letters to Barbara. My spirit was alive with anticipation. The week was going to be so much fun. Barbara knew Memphis; I could count on that, so I always felt safe with her.

I placed my sack of clothes in the closet in the room shared by Janet, one of Barbara's three younger siblings, and Barbara.

"Okay," Barbara said, "tomorrow we will do a few things close to home. Let's do some shopping at the Sterling Store," she enthusiastically spoke.

Of course, shopping at Sterling's would be great but I wanted to be sure to save plenty of my money for our trip to downtown Memphis. We did a lot of things the earlier part of the week but golly, the time was flying by. That is always the way it is when you are having fun, even going to the washeteria for Agnes was made to be fun.

Barbara had two older sisters, Jean and Nancy. Jean was the oldest of Agnes' children. I admired her so much. She had beautiful blond hair. She could easily be a movie star, in my opinion. She was dating, so it was always exciting to watch the guy come to the door to pick her up. Of course, Jean looked gorgeous. I often wondered where they went because I knew that 'city life' was so different to 'country life'.

On Thursday, the big day to go downtown came. Barbara and I could not have been any more excited. Agnes made sure that we understood the rules and then we were off.

Overton Bus #23 pulled into the bus stop. My heart was pounding. This was new to me, of course, I had ridden a school bus but this seemed so different. I stepped up on the big dark gray step, following closely behind Barbara because I did not know what on earth I was doing. I watched as she placed the quarter in the slot that paid for a ride on the bus. I did the same and then we selected our seats. I felt so grown up, but naïve. I watched as we passed areas of Memphis which I had never seen, coming ever closer to downtown. The big bus pulled onto Main Street.

"This is it, Delta, come on let's get off," she told me as she pulled the cord which let the driver know someone wanted off at the bus stop.

"What do you say we go to Woolworth's and shop first," she suggested; so we did.

The store was very big. It had everything you could possibly want to buy. I brought some bobby pins, a hair conditioner, and nail polish, the total coming to $1.15. I had already spent $3.00 of my money and I knew we were going to see a show, eat, shop some more, plus take the bus ride back. Therefore, I needed to keep track of all I was spending. I put back a quarter for the bus ride home, just to make sure I had that.

"Jean said that the best place to eat is at the diner at Kress Drug Store," Barbara recommended.

Jean should know because she works there. We arrive at the drugstore and take a seat at the counter, giggling to each other because a cute guy was working behind the soda counter. We look over the plastic menu of all the items to choose from. We acted so grown up. We both ordered a cheeseburger,

French fries and a chocolate milkshake. The food could not have tasted any better. Barbara takes a look at her watch and declares we had better speed up to make the movie on time.

Sliding off the round red stool, I noticed a small drop of blood which shocked me.

"Barbara, I think I must go to the ladies' room," I said, pointing toward the floor.

"Sure, let's go," she replied. She showed me how to buy a sanitary napkin from the machine located in the ladies' room. Confident that the problem was solved, we started down the street.

The sun was shining so brightly. We passed by so many shops with so much in them that we could buy, if only we had the money. Then we arrived at the Malco Theater where we would see the movie, *The Graduate*.

"What a great show," we both said in a synchronized fashion as we walked back out into the sunlight.

"Hurry, Delta, we do not want to miss our bus home," Barbara said, grabbing my arm and pulling me forward. We repeated the steps from the earlier bus ride, only in the reverse order.

"We are home, Mother," Barbara called out as we both rushed over to the window air conditioner to cool off. We looked at each other and laughed as our hair blew up toward the ceiling.

I was feeling nauseated, so I excused myself to go to the bathroom. It must be the bus ride that was making me feel this way, I thought to myself.

After I sat down on the toilet, I noticed there was no blood on the napkin I had applied. I began to think, I have not had a period the last two months, my weight gain, all my nausea and my mood swings. I leaned over the sink and vomited. I stared at the face in the mirror. I am pregnant. This is just too much for one person to handle, I thought. I guess when I made my exit out of the bathroom something was written all over my face because when I saw Barbara, she immediately said, "What is wrong?"

We went back to her room and I began to tell her the story of what had happened on the day that Mavis had her baby. She immediately grabbed hold of me and we both wept and wept.

"Barbara, that is not all, if only it could end there," I shared as I looked into her red-streaked eyes. "I believe I am pregnant," I confessed.

"Delta, why do you think that?" she questioned.

I gave her all the information as to the reasons why and once again, tears were rolling out of our eyes.

"What, oh, what am I going to do, Barbara?" Delta asked.

"Delta, we need to talk to Mother about this," she replied.

"Barbara, what in the world would she think of me?" I questioned.

"Delta, Mother will not judge you. You have nothing to be judged for. What happened to you was not your fault; no part of this is your fault. So, just get that out of your head and I mean right now," she stated all the while holding me by the shoulders and looking dead into my eyes. She meant business.

That night we called Agnes aside to tell her the whole story and Barbara was right for she did not judge me. As a matter of fact, I felt as though a giant burden had been lifted from my shoulders, even though I still had the greatest disclosure of my life in front of me, telling my beloved Daddy and Mama the truth of what was and is.

Chapter Seven

Confessions

As the miles drew closer and closer, I was trying to mentally plan out the right words to say to Daddy and Mama. My biggest fear was being a disappointment to them. These were my parents, the two most precious people in the world to me. I hated the words, 'rape' and 'pregnant', yet these were the dreadful words which were soon to come out of my mouth.

"Mama, Daddy, we are here," Agnes called out seemingly to an empty house. But here, Daddy and Mama came from the back porch. They were shucking corn and shelling some butter beans. They were so very glad to see us. Both of them hugged me as if I had been gone a month.

"What did you buy, Delta?" Mama questioned with eagerness.

"I brought mostly some personal items for my hair but I have got you and Daddy something," I stated as I pulled out a handkerchief for Mama and a new pair of black shoelaces for Daddy.

Mama fixed us up with a great supper with food that had come from our garden. She was a wonderful cook. Life's lessons had taught her well. Growing up she lived with her daddy, mama, and eight brothers. She was only eleven years old when her Mama died, but from this experience, she grew to become a wonderful cook and homemaker.

"Mama, Daddy, how about we go sit out under the big oak tree," Agnes suggested, "because we have some things to discuss."

"Barbara, you and Delta go set up the chairs and we will be out shortly," Agnes said, motioning to us with her hands to move along. In no time we were all seated under the tree. I cleared my throat.

"Daddy, Mama, you remember the day Mavis' baby, James Earl, was born," so my story began. "While you were gone a terrible thing happened to me. I went to the garden to pick the vegetables and when I returned, Jerry Bennett was inside the house, along with two other guys... Of course, as you can imagine, it caught me totally by surprise." By this time tears were rolling down my face. "Oh, God in Heaven, I wish I did not have to tell you this!" I was crying so hard but trying to get the words out.

"They raped me," I spoke while bawling. By this time my head was nearly in my lap due to the agony of saying the words.

Daddy jumped up and began to cuss, "I am going to kill these son-of-a-bitches one at a time!" Then he headed toward the house.

"Oh, dear Jesus, Agnes, Mama," my eyes moving from one to the other, "one of you must do something," I pleaded. I hated Jerry in the worst way but I did not want my Daddy behind bars for murder.

As we entered the door, we could hear the clicks of the shells as each one was placed in the chamber as Daddy loaded the gun.

"Please, Daddy, put that thing away. You can't do this. It

will only make matters worse. What will happen to us if you are in jail? You mean the world to me. I won't lose you over Jerry Bennett. I just won't. I would rather die first."

"Delta, don't you understand, these boys have hurt the dearest person to me… you. How can I let this pass? They are going to answer for it; this shotgun should end Jerry's worthless life," he said as he walked out the back door.

I ran towards the front door. I knew a shortcut through the field. I ran as hard as I could to get there, doing my dead level best to get there before Daddy. I could hardly breathe because I was crying so hard. Mr. Bennett was chopping wood and I ran right into him as I came around the corner. I screamed, "Get Jerry out of here. Daddy is going to kill him!"

"What the hell, girl," he said, totally confused.

"He raped me, along with two of his buddies. Jerry is a dead man if Daddy gets to him!" I spoke while dragging him by the arm towards the house.

Just then Daddy drove up and jumped out of the truck. You could not help but hear the sound coming from his shotgun as it was locked and loaded. He walked into the front room where, by this time, every Bennett in the place was standing in astonishment. Jerry was standing right in front of them all. Daddy drew a dead aim, his shotgun pointed directly towards Jerry. Quickly, without so much as a thought, I found myself standing in front of Jerry.

"Daddy, you will have to kill me first and if you do you will also kill your unborn grandchild," I cried out. "What is done is done, so put the gun away," I yelled from the depths of my soul.

Immediately Delta turned around to Jerry. "What you took from me was deplorable. Yes, I wish you and your buddies were dead for the pain and terror you have caused me and my family; however, not if it means losing my Daddy because he would go to jail. I am not going to let that happen."

Daddy dropped to his knees. I had only seen Daddy cry one other time, when his Mama died, but now the front of his shirt was wet with tears. I rushed to comfort him. He took his handkerchief from his pocket and wiped his face, seeming a bit embarrassed for breaking down.

"Delta, from this immoral bastard," he said pointing directly at Jerry, "you are having a child?" He had a questionable look on his face, hoping that he had misheard.

"Yes, Daddy, I am pregnant and yes, before you ask, I am going to keep my baby," I declared, even astonishing myself.

"Jerry Bennett, you have not heard the last of this," he said, grabbing him by the collar.

After losing the grip he had on Jerry, he caught me by my hand and said, "Come on, Delta."

We headed out the door.

As soon as the door had shut, Jerry's dad, Rob, jerked Jerry up and held him against the wall.

Rob said, "Boy, if there is any truth to what that gal just said, then you had better keep it to yourself. When the sheriff comes snooping around, asking any questions, you had just better say that you have no notion of what that gal is saying, 'cause you have never touched her. I am glad me and your mama only had boys, 'cause if you had a sister, you probably would have your way with her. Now, Billy Joe, Wayne, let this be a lesson to you, daylight should not catch you with your pants down. You sons-of-bitches, get out of here and do some work for a change."

Rob went to the kitchen.

Words were not spoken during the short trip home. Just as soon as we arrived at the house, Daddy headed towards the barn.

After seeing the expression on Mama's face as I walked into the house, I knew Agnes had told her about the baby. I reached out for her and she immediately pulled me close. I could feel the comfort coming from her and generating through my very soul.

"What happened at Bennett's house?" Mama questioned; I told her everything. "Daddy has gone to be alone and take it all in, I guess. He told Jerry that he will pay. Mama, do you think Daddy will let me keep my baby?" I asked.

"Delta, we will have to go see Sheriff Miller about this whole thing. What Jerry did to you is a wrong and sinful act. Don't you want justice?" Mama spoke with more authority than I had ever seen in her.

"Yes, Mama, I stand for what is right but a lot of time has passed since that day. What do you think Sheriff Miller can do?" I asked, but I kept vocalizing my thoughts, "Is he a miracle worker? All three of them will deny it and stand up for each other. Do you think that he can change or make any difference is this 'darn' rape?" There, Delta said it, but to Mama, she had just cursed.

"Now, young lady, I do not want to hear that kind of language, do you understand me?" she demanded with the sternest of looks that Delta could almost see the little black arrows darting from those baby blue eyes of hers.

"I apologize, Mama, but how much more can I handle?" she questioned, knowing all along she wanted to say… damned RAPE, no matter what Mama thought. But she respected and loved Mama deeply so as not to be so bold. "I need some time to think," she said as she excused herself from the group.

She found herself drifting back to a simpler time when life on the farm was not nearly so intense. Barbara and Nancy were 'city girls' and, at times, had some difficulty in understanding why we wore the clothes we did to hoe cotton. Mama always had our 'hoeing-cotton-garb' which consisted of one of Daddy's long-sleeved khaki shirts, and a pair of his well-worn pants; this, of course, was to protect our skin from the burning of the sun. We were covered from the top of our heads to the bottom of our shoes.

But one day Nancy made a declaration. "If it was me, I would be out here chopping cotton in my swimsuit. That way, I would get all the sun. Boy, would I have a tan!" she said.

Then again, in 'city girl' fashion, she did not understand that she might get a tan only after she had been hauled to the emergency room due to heatstroke. A smile came to Delta's face just thinking about Nancy's carefree thoughts!

She was brought back to reality by hearing Daddy as he walked through the back door and immediately stated, "Delta, come here and go get in the truck. We are going to the sheriff's office."

I knew this was one of those times not to question him. With me and Daddy inside, the truck headed toward town.

"Howdy, Sheriff," Daddy said as he shook Sheriff Miller's hand. "We have a problem, and we need your help."

"What might that be, Earl," the sheriff questioned.

"Straight out, Sheriff, Delta was raped by Jerry Bennett and two other guys. I want them behind bars, before I kill one or all of them," Daddy spoke, all the while reaching for a chair to sit down.

Sheriff Miller opened his desk drawer, pulled out a form and began writing as he asked questions — date, time, how it happened, etc.

"Earl, I understand where you are coming from, but I just can't see how this will not be Delta's word against these three guys; after all, some time has passed since the alleged incident. I am just calling it the way I see it. Now I will bring Jerry in for questioning as soon as we are finished here, but I can't hold him long without some evidence that he committed this alleged raped."

"Alleged rape? I am sick of hearing alleged rape, goddammit, Sheriff, Delta is pregnant. Now you tell me, is this an alleged baby?" Now you tell me, which one of the three fathered this baby? We sure as hell don't know."

By this time, Daddy was back on his feet, walking toward the sheriff. Surely, Daddy knows better than to touch the sheriff, I thought to myself.

"Sit your ass down, Earl, this is my office, at least until the voters tell me otherwise. Anyways, I am on your side. I know those Bennett boys are trouble with a capital T but I must go by the law, you know that.

Again, where is there any evidence that I can put my hands on? Why, these boys will just deny that there is a baby because there was no rape. I don't like pointing this out to you but that's what they will do. Do you want Delta to put through a trial of this nature, Earl?" he questioned. "Never mind," Sheriff Miller continued before Daddy had a chance to speak, "I will run him in for questioning to scare the shit out of him, at least." He said this with what was the first bit of ease during the whole visit.

"I'll come by your place in a day or so," he said as he

showed us to the door. "Take care, Delta."

I nodded my head with a confirmed, yes. Daddy and I drove over to the city grill and ordered us two cheeseburgers and a cold drink. I could not help but see the stress on Daddy's face; nonetheless, he always amazed me with his unconditional love.

"What doctor do you want to see? Will Dr. Leake do it? Let's go on over and let him check you out," Daddy said in a milder tone than I had heard all day.

Sure enough, Dr. Leake said that I was around three months along.

"You should take these vitamins every day and come back to see me in a month," he instructed.

"Yes, sir, I will," I spoke as I was reaching for the door.

There had been so much on my mind lately that I had scarcely had time to think about Bill and what he was doing. I guess by now he has met someone else and I am just a memory. Anyway, when he hears of my condition, I will definitely be history for him I thought.

Two days later there was a knock on the door. It was Sheriff Miller.

"Pesh, good day to you, I have come to talk to Earl and Delta. Are they here?" he asked.

"They are out back. I will go get them. Sheriff, now you make yourself right at home. I'll get you some tea or coffee when I get back," she said with her hospitable voice.

"Earl, Sheriff Miller is here to see you and Delta," Mama said all the while turning to head back to the house.

"Earl, Delta," he started the conversation out as he took a sip of coffee, "it is like I said it would be when I brought the Bennett boy in. The boy denies ever being near Delta. He said

71

she was a whore, his words, not mine, he stressed, and that he would not touch her. I don't like repeating it but that is what came out of his mouth. What do you suggest I do?" Sheriff Miller asked, looking straight up at Delta.

"Sheriff, if it is all the same to Daddy, I would just as soon drop this whole thing. I do not believe they would admit what they did to me. I know, God knows, and Daddy and Mama believe me; that is all that matters to me."

"Are you going to have the baby?" he asked.

"This baby is a part of me. Yes, I realize that I will never know who the father is; I can't change that. However, as best as I can, I plan on raising my baby," I replied in a no-holds-barred fashion.

"Earl, I want to know what you are thinking," Sheriff Miller asks, by this time he is sitting on the edge of the chair.

"Well, let's do it Delta's way. But all I have to say is I better not see Jerry Bennett anywhere near Delta or I will blow what little brains he has straight out of his head," Daddy responded. "Delta is one of my daughters who I love dearly and I will defend her."

Chapter Eight

Keith Anderson Stone

Keith was awakened from a deep sleep by their barnyard rooster crowing. Was what he had experienced weeks ago with Delta real? He reached for his blue jeans and, sure enough, there was her phone number. Thoughts rushed through his head like lightning bolts as to what to do next.

Oh, yea, dinner with Mr. Earl and his wife, Emma. In these parts, she was well known, not by Emma but by Pesh. Ms. Pesh that's what I am going to call her, he concluded.

I wonder if Mr. Earl thought to mention the Sunday dinner to Ms. Pesh, he thought. Keith was itching to call Delta.

Keith's family had lived in Independence for some three to four generations. He did not know anywhere else. They owned a small ranch somewhere around two hundred acres in this hill country.

His daddy, Bobby Gene, was a respected man and proud of it. That is something he wanted for his children — the importance of having a good name.

Keith was every bit of his 6' 1" stature; due to his work around the ranch, he had developed quite a muscular body. When he took his shirt off his tan, and masculine body made him a seriously handsome man. He had just turned twenty-five years old and from working on the ranch, he had managed to save up a nice nest egg.

It was his plan to one day build a cabin in this perfect spot behind the small lake that ran behind their back field. He hoped that it would not be long before his dreams would come true.

He wanted the perfect girl to become his wife. He wished things would work out with Delta because he was fiercely attracted to her. He wondered what in the world she thought of him or, for that matter, did she even think of him at all.

"Son," he could hear his Daddy calling from the kitchen, "get on up for we have some things that need some attention."

Keith slipped on his clothes and walked into the kitchen. Katie, his mother, had baked some fine, hot biscuits and he sat down at the table to butter up about three. After the butter had melted, he poured some molasses all over the open-faced biscuits. Now, add some pieces of sausage to that and you have a fine breakfast.

Drinking his last bit of coffee, he put on his cowboy hat and was ready to take on whatever his dad would put before him.

"Keith," Katie said, "it almost slipped my mind but Mr. Earl called this morning and asked if you could join them for this Sunday dinner."

Mama did not know it, but that was music to his ears. "Mama, will you give them a call back, and let them know that I would be happy to be there on Sunday. Please just find out the time," Keith spoke as he began to head outside to join his dad.

Katie was right behind him. "Young man, you get right back here this minute," she demanded. "If there is any calling to do, you will go right back inside and do it yourself. Do I look like your receptionist?" Katie questioned.

"No Mama, I apologize. I did not mean for it to come out like that," Keith calmly replied.

"Your dad can just hold his horses for this short amount of time," she continued to proclaim.

Keith pulled the weathered piece of paper from his pocket and dialed the number. Mr. Earl answered the phone.

"Mr. Earl, this is Keith Stone. Do you remember me, sir?" Keith questioned.

"Why, sure I do. We want to invite you over for Sunday dinner if it is something you would like to do," Mr. Earl informed him.

"Oh, yes sir, that is why I am calling. That is to accept your invitation and to let you know that I will be looking forward to it, sir," Keith continued.

"Then we will see you around noon or thereabouts," Mr. Earl said.

"Yes, sir, I will be there. Thank you and Ms. Pesh for inviting me. Please let Delta know that I am looking forward to seeing her too," Keith said, but he did not believe it came out the way he wanted it to. "Bye now, sir."

"Dang it, Mama, sometimes things just don't come out of my mouth right," he said. "I am going to work with dad." Katie heard the back door slam behind him.

Man, what a feeling. I am going to get to see Delta on Sunday, more specifically, this Sunday! His day could not have started off any better. Once again, he felt like there was nothing that Daddy could throw at him that he could not handle.

Upon reaching the barn, his opinion began to change. Today was going to be branding day for the cattle. Keith absolutely hated branding. He wished on this day that his big brother, John, was home from the U.S. Army.

"Is that you, Keith?" his dad called out.

"Yes, sir, but you know how I hate this," Keith spoke while taking his hat off because he knew that during the capturing of the cattle it would fall off, and most likely be ruined in the process.

"Son, the cattle must be branded; you know that. I cannot do it alone. So just rise to the occasion and let's get this done," Bobby sternly proposed.

"Okay, Dad, I will go saddle up Ranger and try to get through this day," Keith said as he reached for the bridle. He whistled for Ranger and within minutes he was there, ready to be saddled up.

Upon returning Bobby had the firewood hot with branding irons heated and ready. Keith rode out toward the cattle to round them up into the confined area, where they could be safely secured while the brand was applied. While this was done for the larger cattle, calves were caught in a cradle which is rotated so that the animal is lying on its side. Nothing about this did Keith like doing, but it was all part of taking care of the farm.

He knew his dad was a pro at handling this, only applying the iron long enough to remove the hair and leave the brand. However, he would be glad when this day was over.

The warm water felt so good running down Keith's tired, dirty body. Lathering up with the soap took the smells of the day away; they drained away with the dirty water.

Keith placed his head on the soft pillow. Gosh, it felt so good. Delta quickly came to mind. He wondered what she was doing. Was she looking forward to Sunday as much as he was? Thoughts of what he should wear also came to mind. I want to look my very best and I know Mama can help me make the right choice of clothes. He always felt that fresh blue jeans worked, with a plaid western shirt, boots, and cowboy hat. He would feel good wearing that.

In his mind, he could just picture Delta with her beautiful brunette hair. He wondered how it would feel to run his fingers through it. Dare he think of such a thing? He envisioned his lips touching her sweet lips. His whole body shivered. He could almost smell the scent of her as he closed his eyes; magnificent warmth fell over his body. He thought of her luscious body and imagined it touching his. What would it be like to actually touch her body and hold it close to his? But he was quickly jolted back to reality when he heard Mama calling him for supper. He would almost forgo eating a meal for thoughts like this.

It was a bright sunny day as Keith's eyes opened and he quickly realized this was the day that he had been waiting to arrive. He took a quick shower, applied the best toilet water he had, combed his hair, dressed, and quickly added another quick shine to his cowboy boots. A man has got to look his best, he thought before heading down to breakfast.

"Good morning, family," he said with happiness resounding in his voice.

"We know what has got you so happy and she lives in Dubbs, Mississippi," Katie gave out a tease.

"Dad, do you think I could use our car, that is if neither of you have any plans for it," he added.

"Sure, Son, I thought you might ask that, so she is all clean and ready for the trip," Bobby answered him. "Just see that you take good care of her and are home at a decent hour."

"I promise both of you because it is just Sunday dinner. I do not suppose Mr. Earl will allow me to take Delta anywhere else, say to the movies? I would like to take her, but this is only the first date, if I can even call it that," Keith replied.

Keith did not eat much at breakfast, only a biscuit with some butter, jam, and some coffee. Then he hurried back upstairs to brush his teeth and get the small bouquet of flowers for Delta. He was going to give Ms. Pesh some peaches which were picked fresh from their trees.

The 1959 Ford Fairlane, the Stone's family car, was pulling into the Daze's driveway at exactly noon.

Keith knew he would be telling a lie if he said that there were not hundreds of butterflies in his stomach but hey, he would be all right because he could count on Mr. Earl to help him out.

Delta greeted him at the front door with Snow, her white cat, in her arms, "Come on in, Keith and make yourself at home. Mama will have dinner ready in just a bit.

"Hi Delta, I thought you might enjoy these flowers," Keith said as he handed the bouquet over to her.

"That is so thoughtful of you, I love them. Thank you so much. I will go place them in some water," she replied as she exited the room.

"Good day, Keith," Mr. Earl said as he shook Keith's right hand. "Now, like Delta said, ``make yourself right at home, that is the way we want you to feel while you are visiting us."

"Yes, sir, Mr. Earl, I will," Keith replied. "Once again, thank you for inviting me to have dinner. You know this is one way for me to get to know Delta better. I do not think that I am fooling you." He knew it went without saying.

Mama and Delta came out of the kitchen. Mama was

removing her apron but always placed it close by.

"Mama, I would like for you to meet our guest, Keith Stone. Keith, this is my Mama, Pesh," Delta introduced them.

"It is my pleasure to meet you, Ms. Pesh. I have something for you, too." He went to the front porch and brought in the peaches. "Here you go. I just know you can make a great peach pie," Keith said as he handed them to her.

"Thank you, Keith, and you are right, we just love fried peach pies. Dinner is ready and I hope that you like chicken and dressing for that is what we are having. Now excuse me while I finish pouring the tea. You do drink tea, don't you?" Mama questioned before leaving.

"Oh, yes, I do. Thank you so much," Keith said. By this time, Mama was almost out of the room.

Everyone gathered at the table. "Ms. Pesh, everything tastes delicious," Keith said.

"Oh, Mama makes the best chicken and dressing in the world," Delta did not hesitate to emphasize. "You will most likely enjoy anything that Mama makes because she is such a good cook."

"What kind of work have you been doing on the Stone farm this week, Keith," Daddy asked. He could not resist farm talk.

"Well, I have to admit we have been doing something that I like the least on a farm — branding our calves and cattle. It is something that my brother, John, doesn't have a problem with so he does it when he is here. However, he is away with the U.S. Army, leaving only me to help Dad. Not that I am complaining about the work, don't get me wrong, I will help my dad out with anything on the farm," Keith stated.

"Don't give it another thought. That is not one of my

favorite things to handle either, but it has to be done," Daddy answered.

Keith was such a polite young man. His mother and father had truly taught him good manners. He seems to know and do what any 'city slicker' in a fancy restaurant would do on a date, pull out the chair, use a napkin properly, say please and thank you, etc.

After dinner was finished, Daddy and Keith went outside for a while. Mama and Delta cleaned the table, stored the leftovers, and washed, dried, and put away the dishes.

After they returned inside, we all watched television for about an hour or so and then Keith invited me to go for a walk. He asked Daddy and Mama if that would be all right with them and, of course, they said, "Yes." We walked down toward the pond located on our land.

"Delta, I do not want to do anything to upset you, but could I hold your hand as we walk?", Keith questioned shyly.

Without a word, Delta reached over and placed her hand in his. He looked pleased.

"Keith, what plans do you have for the future?" Delta questioned.

"Honestly, Dad gives me a salary for helping him on the farm and I am doing everything I can to save so I can have a cabin built on this special plot of land on our farm. I show more interest in the farm than John does, so I will probably work there until — gosh, I do not know when, until I die maybe," Keith said and laughed out loud because to say 'until I die' at his young age just seemed funny.

"What about you, Delta, are you going away to college?" Keith asked with great interest.

"To be honest, I am not sure. I have the grades that are

needed to get into college but I truly do not believe that Daddy and Mama can afford to send me, so I will probably just find a job. There are not that many jobs around this area. Nevertheless, I am certain if a girl puts her mind to it, she could find one. Judy, my best friend, and I have talked about moving to Clarksdale to find a job and a small apartment; I really do not think that either of our parents like that idea. So truthfully, I will just be living here at home, helping out at the farm and working somewhere, if possible," Delta said, seemingly not taking a breath in between words.

They arrived at the pretty little pond, found a suitable place to sit down on the bank, and began watching nature as it disappeared and reappeared.

Delta could not get over how she had overlooked how handsome he was on the day they met at the ranch. His curly brown hair was so neatly combed, his beautiful blue eyes could lead you into a trance and his dimples made him so charming. Of course, she had not seen what was underneath his clothing; however, she felt certain it could make her heart skip a beat.

"You have the most beautiful hair, Delta. It looks so shiny and soft," Keith said, wondering if the words came out right and what to do or say next. He wanted to touch it but he was nervous to be so bold as to just do so, or to even ask.

"Thank you. I try to condition it to keep it healthy; I do thank you for saying so," Delta replied.

At that moment, without forethought, their eyes met and instantaneously their lips moved closer and closer until they touched. Inside Keith's mind, he was in Heaven; at the very least, he believed not too many things on earth got much better. Delta's heart was beating faster and faster. It seemed like the longer they kissed, the faster it became. She could feel her body responding to the sheer passion of their kissing. He gently lowered her head back and the moment continued. Keith certainly did not want it to end; if Delta was questioned, she did not either. She loved what she was feeling. She certainly respected the man and did not want the moment to end. The embrace broke but they remained frozen in time.

They heard someone calling but they did not understand what was going on. It was not dark and they had not been gone for a terribly long time. It was Daddy calling Keith.

Keith stood up so he could better understand what Mr. Earl was saying. "Keith, your dad just called, he and Katie are taking your grandmother, Virginia, to the hospital in Senatobia. He told me to tell you to meet them there," Daddy concluded.

"Yes, sir, I will be right there," Keith spoke all the while reaching to lift Delta. They hurried back to the house.

Keith told them what a wonderful time he had had. He thanked Ms. Pesh for the wonderful meal and asked Delta to follow him to his car, which she did.

"Delta, just as soon as Grammy is okay, would you be my date for a movie?" Keith asked.

"I would enjoy that and we will just as soon as you know the condition of your grandmother. Now you go and take care of your family and let me know what is wrong; if I can help, please let me know," she said insistently.

"I will, I promise. Thank you, thank you for today," he said as he turned the car engine on.

Delta watched until the Ford was no longer in her vision and she went inside.

Although the drive to the hospital was only about twenty miles, it was a long ride for Keith because of his great concern for his grammy. He put the car in park, turned the engine off, and ran inside the hospital.

"Where is Virginia Stone?" he spat out the question to the first person he saw behind a desk, nurse or not. She checked her listing and said that she was still in the Emergency Room but should be assigned a room shortly.

"What's wrong with her?" Keith seemed stressed as he blurted out the question.

"I am sorry, sir, but you will have to wait to speak to the doctor or a member of the family who is with her," the lady replied calmly.

Keith took a seat in the hope that it would not be long before his mama or dad would appear. Such enough, he had just gotten comfortable as his parents walked into the room.

"How is Grammy, what is wrong with her?" he quickly questioned.

"She has pneumonia in one lung but the doctor said that after a short hospital stay and treatment, she should be fine," Bobby said with a matter-of-fact attitude.

"When can I see her? I want her to know that I am here. Take me back there, Dad," Keith nervously responded.

"Son, I know how you feel but let the doctors and nurses do what they need to do and get her to her room; then we will all go up there," Bobby replied.

After about thirty minutes, the family was told that Mrs. Stone had been taken to room #246. They gathered their things and headed up to see her.

Keith could not get there quick enough. "Grammy, I have been so worried," he said as he held her hand.

"Dad, she looks so pale. I do not think I have ever seen anyone that white. I am worried. Is she getting air?" questions were coming from Keith's mouth faster than anyone could answer.

Doctor Spencer walked into the room. "Hello all, this young lady has, as you already know, pneumonia in the right lung. The good news is that it has been discovered in the early stage. Now whether she will require artificial ventilation in the early stage is difficult to predict. It most likely will be needed, due to Mrs. Stone's age. Do you understand? She has a fever, which we will be monitoring. After we receive the results from the tests we have ordered, the best treatment will be made. The medical staff will try their best to treat her and get her back home and out of this place. I will keep you updated as we know more. Are there any questions?" he asked.

I guess we're still trying to absorb what all had just been said to us since we did not really know what questions to ask; we just thanked him and he left the room.

"Grammy, this sure is a nice room," Keith said in an effort to comfort her. She seemed to find the strength to reach over and pat his hand. He wished he knew how to help her but truly just being there was plenty.

It was decided that Katie would stay the night since Bobby and Keith could best take care of all of the animals' needs the next day. Anyway, Katie felt Ginny, as she called her, would feel best if she were there.

The ride home was a quiet one. "Sure is a pretty night sky," Keith finally broke the silence.

"Yes, Son, it sure is. You and I had better turn in early tonight for we have a good many things to take care of before we head back to the hospital to see Mama," Bobby spoke with concern in his voice.

Bobby turned the engine off and the two men started for

the front door. "Dad, do mind if I take a minute out at the stables," Keith questioned.

"No, take all the time you need, Son. I understand," Bobby said as he turned to give his son a hug.

Keith went to his room, grabbed his guitar and went through the kitchen into the back porch and out the back door. He reached the big cattle gate then leaned his arm across the big post and looked toward the heavens.

Tears were dripping off his face as he began his prayer, "Our God in Heaven, it is an old country boy talking to you now. You already know what is in my heart for you to see; it is my grammy. I have never seen her look so pale. If I said that I was not scared, I would not be telling you the truth for I don't want to lose this special lady. Lord, if it is her time, then I know that she would be the first to say to you, let it be, for she is a fine Christian woman. You would be blessed to have her Home but Lord, I am being selfish now; please, please spare my grammy and bring her home to us. Your will is what I pray for and not my will be done. It is a special request from her youngest grandson. You see I love her and she has yet to have any of her grandchildren have any children for her to love. I want that for her because I know she wants that as well. So, God, please, should it be your will, spare her for us. Give her health back and let us bring her home. I thank you, too, for the wonderful time I have today with Delta and her family. You certainly blessed me there. So, it is with a humble heart that I speak with you and it is in Your son's name, Jesus, that I request this. Amen."

Keith picked up his guitar and began singing *Amazing Grace,* for that was one of Grammy's favorite songs. Keith was a fine country singer. He sang at church and county fairs mostly. He did not believe that Delta had ever heard him sing but he had plans for that to change. He wanted to be thinking more about Delta but right now he had such a heavy heart.

It's hard not to think of her, even now with so much crowding his brain, thoughts of her creep in. He can see her beautiful face. Oh, how he wished he was looking into her eyes. He knew there was something special about Delta from the moment he laid eyes on her. He just had to find a way to be with her.

I have to shake this… There would be other times that he would rejoice to have her on his mind; he just had to somehow shake it right now. He heard Ranger snicker in his stall. Dad always made certain that the animals were placed in a safe place for from time to time a panther or two had been known to come through these parts. He started for the stall. He would give Ranger some attention. Maybe that could take his mind off all the things whirling in his brain.

Keith was unaware that his dad was only several yards away from him, standing next to the barn, not that he was eavesdropping. He just did not want to be alone. Bobby was so proud of his son. He would not make his presence known for he knew this was a special time between Keith and God. It took everything in him not to run to his son to hold him and weep in his arms, but he quietly strolled back to the house and began getting ready to face whatever tomorrow might bring.

The Stone Family lived in a country house on a two-hundred-acre tract of land. They were proud and honest people and treated others the same. Bobby and Katie had always taught their two sons to love their country and, by all means, treat a lady with respect. They were proud of their boys. One, John, was serving his country in the U.S. Army, and the other,

Keith, had chosen to remain on the farm to help his dad. Both were handsome young men. In disposition, John took after his dad and, as it usually happens, Keith took after his mom. Keith had light brown curly hair and when he smiled, two distinct dimples appeared. They, like most people in this part of the country, grew cotton and soybeans. The rich Delta land generally grows fine crops. Cattle was also something that Bobby liked having on his farm.

Bobby and Keith turned in early. Keith certainly had Grammy on his mind but he also lay awake thinking about Delta. In his mind, he could picture her beautiful face being framed by her beautiful dark hair. She had a peaches and cream complexion and a captivating smile. He closed his eyes so he could better remember when his lips touched hers; it caused warmth to drift over his body. He thought this is the woman I want to marry, for he knew he was falling deeply in love with her; with those thoughts, he drifted off to sleep.

Chapter Nine

Time with Grammy

Delta was up early today because she wanted to finish whatever Daddy and Mama had planned for her to do. That way, she could drive to the hospital to visit Mrs. Stone. She dressed, made the bed and cleaned her room; then she started into the kitchen for breakfast.

"Good morning, Daddy and Mama," she said as she gave them a morning hug. "I need to know what all you have for me to do because if it is all right with you, I want to go visit Mrs. Stone at the hospital."

Mama was the first to speak, "Just gather the eggs and feed the chickens, dogs and cats. I guess that is all I need you to attend to."

"All of that is fine with me," Daddy said. "Just make sure you eat a good breakfast because it sounds like you are going to be in for a long day."

Delta never quite understood it, but Daddy was always stressing eating a good breakfast. Oh well, maybe he did not have good food to eat back in the depression days in which he grew up. Whatever the reason, she just took him at his word and sat down to help her plate.

"I wonder what is wrong with Mrs. Stone," Mama asked. "It must be something serious for them to place her in the hospital."

"I am sure Keith will give me a call soon to let us know because I asked him when he left yesterday." Delta had only gotten the words out of her mouth when the telephone rang. "I will get it," she quickly said.

"Hello," Delta said.

"Delta, this is Keith. I wanted to call and let you know how Grammy is doing. She has pneumonia, Dr. Spencer told us. Mama spent the night at the hospital and Dad and I will be going back up there later today after we finish the things we have to do on the farm," Keith said nonstop.

"Thank you so very much for letting us know because we were wondering how she was doing just before your call," Delta told him and continued with a question. "Keith, do you mind if I stop by later at the hospital to visit your grandmother?" she questioned.

"Heavens, no, I do not mind. I think that it is kind of you," Keith answered with joy in his voice. "We will be back over at the hospital this afternoon; I just can't say a time because we have to get our work done. I hope I see you while you are there."

"I hope to see you too," Delta replied. "Well, I had better finish up here so that I can get to the hospital. Bye, Keith."

Delta drove into the parking lot at about three thirty that afternoon. She did not know Mrs. Stone but she was certainly looking forward to getting to know her. She knocked on the hospital door. A lady came to open the door.

"Yes, may I help you?" Katie questioned.

"My name is Delta Daze and I am a friend of Keith. I learned that his grandmother was here in the hospital and I would like to pay her a visit, if you do not mind," Delta answered.

"Oh, no, no, I do not mind a bit. Come on in," Katie said as she showed her to a chair.

The elderly lady lying in the bed looked so ill. Delta had never seen anyone look so pale. "What do the doctors say?" she asked.

"They are very concerned about the fever. They have been trying to get it under control but I guess it is there to help her fight off this infection," Katie concluded.

"Delta, do you mind sitting with Ginny while I go get a bite to eat at the diner?" Katie asked.

"I do not mind one bit. You go eat. I brought a book or two for I thought that she might enjoy me reading to her," Delta said.

Katie left. Delta got out the book of poems which she enjoyed so she felt certain Mrs. Stone would like them, too. She began to read. In a few minutes, Mrs. Stone opened her eyes and turned to find where the sound was coming from. At first, she looked puzzled; then asked, "Do I know you?"

"No, but I want you to know me. My name is Delta, Delta Daze and I am a friend of your grandson, Keith. I know you are so proud of him for he is such a nice man." Delta just kept talking. "Is it all right if I read to you? I thought that you might enjoy these poems. I sure do."

Mrs. Stone said nothing more. She just nodded her head yes and closed her eyes.

Delta's voice was soft as she read the words from the pages. She could not help but believe the frail pale lady was enjoying each poem being read to her.

Katie arrived back in the room. "Now, how did you and Keith meet?" she asked.

"My daddy, Earl Daze, bought me a horse and Keith was at the ranch helping me as I rode them. Daddy invited him to Sunday dinner that has just passed. As a matter of fact, that is where Keith was when he learned that Mrs. Stone had taken ill," Delta said.

"Keith is our youngest son and, of course, as his mom, I am proud of him. He works with his dad on the farm. His older brother, John, is in the U.S. Army," said Katie.

"Yes, Keith told me that and, yes, I can tell he is a fine young man. I am anxious to get to know him better," Delta spoke, hoping Mrs. Stone did not believe her to be pushy.

At that moment the door opened. and Bobby and Keith walked into the room. Katie got up and hugged both of them. Delta watched as Keith came over and as he did, she stood up and he hugged her. She felt so pleased that he had made this gesture.

"How are you, Delta?" Keith asked as he squeezed her hand ever so slightly.

"I am doing just fine but I believe Mama and Daddy will be expecting me home pretty soon and I know you want some time with your grandmother. With that, she kissed Keith on the cheek, said her goodbyes and left for home.

Delta pulled into the drive and picked up the bag of groceries that she had purchased at the Kroger store.

When she entered the room, Mama was ironing her Daddy's clothes just as she always does. Daddy was peeling some potatoes for supper. Daddy made fried potatoes just like his mama had taught him and, boy, were they good! Delta met each of them with a hug and a kiss.

"Oh, Daddy, my mouth is already watering for some of those "Daze" potatoes," Delta said with a grin. She knew

Daddy loved people to brag about his fried potatoes.

"How is Keith's grandmother doing?" Mama asked.

"Mama, she looks so very pale and the doctors are concerned about the high fever," Delta said, all the while putting away the groceries. "The doctors are giving her medicines to treat her and we all need to keep her in our prayers," Delta concluded.

"Oh, Mama, you have cooked some pinto beans. You make the best pinto beans in the whole wide world. I just can't wait for supper. What can I do to help?" Delta asked.

"Go ahead and stir the beans. I would like for us to have some cornbread. If you wanted to, you could make that," Mama suggested.

Without hesitation, Delta took the bowl from the cabinet, found the ingredients and began making the cornbread.

Daddy was busy preparing his potatoes to fry up. Delta could hear them as they were dropped into the sizzling grease. Oh, she knew they were in for some good food tonight.

After supper, Delta insisted that Mama go to the living room to watch some television; she would clean up the kitchen. Daddy stuck around to help.

"Delta, tell me if I am getting into your business but your dresses are starting to get a bit tight," Daddy hesitantly said.

"I know, Daddy. A friend of Peggy's is going to lend me some of her maternity clothes for we are the same size. I just have not picked them up yet; I will soon, I promise," Delta replied.

Daddy loved his little girl and was so afraid of what troubles she was facing because people were going to talk. What was she going to say to Bill and Keith? He did not know which guy Delta liked the most but either way, it was not going to be an easy task.

"I see you worrying, Daddy. Now you stop that right now. I will be all right. You will see. Come on, let's go watch some television with Mama. She is probably lonesome," Delta said as she caught her Daddy by the hand.

"Those are the funniest shows. It is so good to laugh. Mama and Daddy, if you do not mind, I am going to go out to the barn and visit Queen for a while," Delta said as she put on her sweater.

Mama looked at Earl and said, "Our baby girl is facing difficult times. I am afraid for her. You know how mean people can be. This is not her fault but they do not know that. You know what they will be thinking; I don't like it but there's nothing I can do about it."

"Pesh, Delta is a smart young lady now and we have to believe that she can handle all of the things she is facing. Certainly, by the grace of God, she can," Earl stressed, all the while being just as worried. Best not to let on to Pesh, he thought.

The stars were shining brightly as Delta walked toward the barn. She stopped to watch the fireflies as each of their tails lit up. How do they do that, she wondered. As she got closer to the barn, she knew Queen sensed her arrival because she could hear her stirring.

"Queen, girl, I have come to see you. It has been a while since I did not get to see you today but I had something important to do. I am going to do it again the day after tomorrow, that is if Mrs. Stone is still in the hospital. I do not want to take time away from her family but if they want me to, I will go every day. You will understand, Queen, my sweet girl. I promise this weekend we will go for a long ride. Maybe, if

Mrs. Stone is better, Keith and I will go fishing. You will like Keith. I just know you will, for he is a good, kind man. Queen, I know you will like him because I like him… Queen, I am going to have a baby. It will be born sometime in December, I think. I have got to go to the doctor soon but to be honest with you, I dread it. We do not want to worry Mama and Daddy, so you have to help me be strong. Queen, what is the best way to handle this? I have got to tell Keith.

"Gosh, Bill has not called or been around for some time now. I wonder if he has heard something about me and the baby. What if he doesn't want anything to do with me? Maybe that is why he hasn't been in touch with me.

"I guess with all that has been going on, I have not had time to think too much about Bill. What is happening, Queen? Do I care more about Keith now? I feel so confused. I did not feel that way when I came out here. I guess when you and I talk everything comes out, all those things that I am afraid to let Mama and Daddy know. I don't want them to worry.

"Queen, I am going to get those clothes from Linda and then face Keith with the truth. It will be Keith first because he has been closest to me. I will tell Bill in due time. I love you so much, Queen, but I had better get back in the house. I will see you again tomorrow."

Delta closed the barn door, looked up toward Heaven and asked God for strength and courage. Please let people somehow understand, even though I know it is asking a whole lot for them to do that. Please, God, let this be my burden and not Mama and Daddy's. They are so good to me and I thank you so very much for giving them to me. I do not want my baby to suffer either. Whether it is a girl or boy, I promise to raise my child to love and trust in You. I love this baby already.

God, please help me.

Delta walked along the path back to the house and came toward Daddy and Mama, as if she did not have a care in the world.

Chapter Ten

Shiloh Trip

Delta's body was filled with adrenaline. She could not wait to see Keith's new car; the car was not actually new, just new to Keith. He had brought a 1966 Chevrolet Malibu convertible. It was red with four on the floor.

Delta heard him drive into the driveway and she dashed out to meet him.

"Hi, beautiful lady," Keith said, leaning forward to place a kiss on her lips.

"Wow, what a beautiful car. I can't wait to ride in it," she said as she rubbed her hands over the white seats.

"Do you have everything ready for our trip to Shiloh?" Keith questioned, knowing all along that Delta always did things in an organized manner.

"You bet I do. We need to go tell Daddy and Mama that we are leaving, plus Daddy will want to see your new car."

"Sorry, Delta, but he has already seen the car. He just happened to be in Dubbs the day I drove her home. I stopped to fill her up and there was Earl."

"You mean my daddy is holding out on me?" she joked.

At the top of the steps, Keith reached down to pet Snow, Delta's snowy white cat. Delta was crazy about Snow and, if Keith were to be totally honest, so was he.

"Hi, Earl," Keith said as he shook his hand. "What kind of week have you had? It's been a hot one, hasn't it?" he asked.

"Oh, you bet it has. We worked all week hoeing out the garden. That surely is a fine-looking car."

"Thank you, sir. I am proud of it. I am going to have 'our girl' most of the day. We are going to drive up to the Military Park in Shiloh, Tennessee. We are planning to have a picnic. I promise to have her home before midnight," he told Mr. Earl.

Mama made her way out of the kitchen. She always enjoyed visiting Keith, even if it was just for a little bit.

"Why, if it is not Pesh, one of the sweetest ladies in this county," Keith comments as he reaches out to hug her.

"Thank you, Keith, I am glad you think I am sweet and do not know the real me," Mama stated knowing full well that being kind and loving were standards she lived by.

"I fried some chicken for your picnic; I hope you enjoy it," Mama kept on talking, not allowing Keith a word in edgewise.

"You bet we will, Pesh, and I appreciate it. Thank you very much for your hard work. Like I told Earl, we will be home before midnight, but, to do that we had best be headed out."

There was hardly a cloud in the sky. Delta was seated right next to Keith. She watched as the wind tossed his curly hair from side to side as they drove along the highway. She could not imagine being with any other man. In every way he completed her and she believed he felt the same way about her. Though he had not mentioned marriage, with all her heart, she believed it would happen one day.

Shiloh Military Park was a good 140 miles from Dubbs and not the easiest of roads to travel.

"How much further before we get there?" she asked, mainly because she was definitely getting hungry for some of that chicken Mama had prepared.

"We are only about five miles away, Ms. Impatient," he said, smiling back at heer, making jis beautiful dimples ever so obvious.

"Oh, you go eat a bug, Keith Anderson Stone, that's what you can do," she spoke as she poked him on his leg.

Keith laughed. Loving every minute of it.

It was so interesting to see the soldier's reenactment of the Battle of Shiloh which occurred on April 6 and 7, 1862. There were 65,000 Union troops and 44,000 confederates. It is recorded that the Battle of Shiloh resulted in nearly 24,000 killed, wounded, and missing. For Delta, one of the most interesting places in the park was the Bloody Pond. It was at this pond that soldiers of both sides bathed their wounds. It is said that their blood stained the water red.

Keith and Delta picked out a great place to have the picnic which was underneath a huge oak tree. This tree must be two hundred years old, she thought. Keith spread out a large quilt that once was his grammys.

"What is that you have?" she questioned him about the bottle of champagne which he just placed in a cooler. "You know, Mama, being the Southern Baptist she is, would never approve of my drinking that," she was hesitant to mention but felt she must.

"Trust me, Delta, your Mama will not have a problem with this." He went back to unloading the car.

"She surely made a lot of fried chicken. There is enough for an army, judging by weight. I love your Mama's cooking. She makes a chocolate pie that is to die for, but I bet there is not one of those under this 'turtle hull'. Keith was speaking almost to himself, for Delta was walking around feeling a wonderful breeze underneath the huge trees, almost transformed into another world.

"Come and get it, dinner is ready," he called to her. Everything was all placed and ready for them to enjoy.

"Doesn't everything taste great?" Delta asked Keith as she wiped her mouth with a napkin.

"You're doggone right, it sure does. We are going to have to do something extra special for Ms. Pesh for cooking all this," Keith responded.

Keith asked Delta to lie back and place her head on his lap. He gently stroked her forehead and gazed into her beautiful face. "Delta, I am going to admit something to you. I am the luckiest man in the world to know you, much less have you as my girl. I like you a whole lot," Keith said."

Those words struck a nerve for Delta. A person can like a lot of things, cars, horses, certainly other people, etc., but they only love certain things. Why had he bothered to talk at all if the best he could do is like me? There was absolutely no doubt in her mind that she was deeply in love with him. She questioned in her mind. Is it that men take a longer time to admit to what is in their heart? Rather, was it that 'like' is exactly all that he felt? He could probably see those hazel eyes of hers dancing as she tried to figure out what in the world 'like you' could mean?

"Did I 'get your goat', Delta Daze? You are a Mississippi Delta beauty, and right now you are '"my beauty."' I have a surprise for you. That is the reason for the champagne."

He took the bottle, uncorked it, and poured just enough in her glass so as not to 'offend' Mama, and poured half a glass in the other. "I propose a toast to us… that our hearts forever be united in a deep, passionate love." With that, their glasses clinked, and they took a drink.

By this time, Delta was doing her dead level best to figure out what Keith was up to. This entire trip had been solely planned by Keith.

Keith took out a little black box. "Delta, I am going to tell you something that I have never told any other woman." He was staring deeply into her beautiful eyes, while he told her, "I love you with all of my heart. I think about you constantly, and I miss you so much when we are a part." He handed her the box. She was shaking inside with anticipation; could it be a ring?

"Go on, girl, open it," Keith insisted.

There was a beautiful heart necklace inside. It had a gorgeous red ruby heart in the center with diamonds surrounding it. At least, Delta knew the stones were not really diamonds or a ruby. She knew full well they were rhinestones; but she loved them just as much.

"Delta, I give you my heart. Will you take it?" he adoringly asked.

Tears streamed down her face as she tried to share with him how long she had known that she was in love with him. "Keith, I believe I fell in love with you on the bank of our pond when you came to our house for Sunday dinner. I wish I could immediately ask you to hook the necklace around my neck but I have something very serious to tell you."

Keith looked so confused because he expected only reactions of joy.

"Keith, I know that you can tell that I am gaining weight because I am. I have a reason to because I am pregnant," she stated all the while watching his eyes. It is not of my design," she went on. It was hard hearing the words come from her mouth and going to his ears. "Keith, I was raped," she stopped to see his reaction.

"Raped by whom?" he asked both with anger and confusion.

"It is a long story but you should know all of the facts. Mavis had gone into labor and Mama, Daddy, and Peggy went to be with her. I do not like being around these kinds of things. I would rather hear about it than be there firsthand, so I pleaded with Daddy and Mama to let me stay at home. I had some studying to do and I just did not want to be there. With reservations, they allowed me to stay. I went to the garden to pick some of the vegetables and, upon coming back into the kitchen, three men were standing right in front of me. I tried to reason with them but they were determined to do what they came to do so they did. I will spare you the horrifying details. I did everything that I could possibly do but I was no match for them.

"After they finally left, I washed and washed my skin until I thought it would bleed. I straightened everything as best as I could and was determined to take this with me to the grave; however, then I learned I was pregnant. I detest these men— no they are not men, they are animals, but I already love this baby that I am carrying.

I know this is a lot for you to absorb and think about; I will understand if you just want to walk away," Delta said all the while weeping almost uncontrollably.

Keith stood up; and ran his fingers through his hair. By this time his face had reddened in anger. "I, too, despise these men who would do such a thing to you. Is it that you do not want to name them? I would like to know. Will you tell me, Delta, please?" Keith was asking but almost pleading.

"Yes, Keith, I believe you have a right to know. One of the men who raped and terrorized me was Jerry Bennett. Nonetheless, after my daddy and Sheriff Miller went to see them, we decided not to press charges. I do not know if that was totally the right thing to do but that is what we did." She stopped talking but he kept looking into her eyes.

"Delta, I believe that I have loved you from the moment that I laid eyes on you. I need some time to think. Please do not get me wrong, I believe you and I know that this is not your fault. It is a situation in which I know calls for bravery and for this I commend you, but I still need to have some time to process this.

She took a few steps back, but was still locked into each other's gaze, she said, "Keith, I have given you so much information. You need time to digest all of it. I want to do whatever I can for you."

"Oh, my goodness, my sweet Delta, you have been placed in an unbelievable state. My heart aches for you. I don't know what else to say at this moment," Keith said, reaching for Delta's hand.

By this time, Delta had turned to look at the beautiful scenery. She was nervous about what Keith was thinking about after all that she told him...

She turned now toward him, clutched his strong hands and spoke directly, "By all means, I understand what you are saying and you certainly deserve all the time you need. I do not want to put you into any situation that you are uncomfortable with. I love you too much to do that to you. Please know that when I decided to have my baby, I understood the gravity of the decision and I took it upon myself. Keith, I want my mama and daddy to be spared as much hurt and anguish as possible. This is mine to deal with, not theirs; though, I know they support me in every way they know how."

Delta tried to ease the tension of the moment as she spoke, "Speaking of Mama and Daddy, we had better pack up all these things and start for home. I do not want to be late."

Keith moved his hands down around Delta's waist and then gently moved them slowly up her soft skin to her neck.

"What a beautiful neck this is; and I want to hook this necklace on it because that is where it belongs. What do you say about that, my sweet Delta?" he asked.

"Please, Keith, I would be honored to wear it," and with those words, she turned so Keith could hook it around her neck.

"I love you so much," he said as he held her close. They gently embraced there under that giant old oak tree where, most likely, soldiers once stood.

"We had better get things together and head out for home," Keith said.

The day has been so much fun so I guess we had best get going," she said hesitantly.

The drive home was a quiet one for they both had a lot to think about. It seemed like a long one too, but Delta could not have asked for any more understanding than what she had received. They drove into the driveway and Keith held her hand as they walked toward the door.

"Please thank Pesh and Mr. Earl for allowing me to have you for the day. I will be in touch with you soon, I promise," he spoke as he pulled her close. "Try not to worry, we will figure this out," and with those words, he went toward the car and drove off.

Delta stood there crying as she rubbed her hands down across her belly and felt the baby move. "Oh, I love you little one," she softly spoke.

Chapter Eleven

Cheyenne Wins the Greenville Rodeo

The big diesel truck backed the four-stall horse trailer right next to the entry gate. It would not be long before all of the equipment needed for the rodeo would be packed neatly into the truck. The horse trailer was as clean as a pin and ready for Cheyenne.

Lawrence had made certain that Bill had a quality riding saddle and all of the equipment. He had learned of a new company, Circle Y, located in Yoakum, Texas which manufactured quality saddles. He wanted Bill to have a design and contour cut which would allow comfort, but also feel close to the horse. He knew that the more Bill was in tune with Cheyenne, the better control of cutting the cattle he had.

Cheyenne understood every movement he was to take when the reins touched his neck; but it was also Bill's responsibility to feel his horse's needs. It was an amazing thing to watch the practice sections as Bill could anticipate Cheyenne's every move, just as Cheyenne anticipated the movement of the cattle. They worked as a perfect team.

This rodeo was located in Oxford, Mississippi. The town was only about eighty miles from Tunica and since it was so close to home, every cowboy with good sense would be entered into some event. Some had good horses, while some needed to work more with their horses to become a better team. As with any event, there would also be guys there who did not know shit from Shinola.

Liz was going to attend this Oxford Rodeo. She and Martha Rose were working on a project, which at the present time, needed them in Tunica. They were working on the October Festival. There was so much production to be done to provide a fun-filled, something-for-everyone event, as well as things that the men were not too embarrassed to participate in. Liz and Martha definitely had their work cut out for them for this event.

Liz had packed some snacks to place in the cab of the truck. She knew that Bill would stop off at a local steakhouse for dinner; a few snacks would come in handy until then. His favorite steakhouse was in Como, Mississippi. She did not see that there would be any difference on this trip.

By this time, Leroy, the Rooster, had strolled over to where Liz was stationed at the truck. He flew up and landed on the steering wheel.

"You silly rooster, you would go if they would let you and probably steal the show," Liz spoke to Leroy.

Leroy was one special rooster. It was almost as though he understood what he was being told. Sometimes he would make noises at Lawrence when he had closed the door. It was as if Leroy thought that he should be up in his arms, going where he was going. He was a rooster with a mind of his own and he didn't mind speaking it! However, here we were with Leroy sitting in a truck, which was going to a place he had no business going.

"Leroy," Liz called, "come on, let's go to the barn to see the baby pigs." Whether he understood or not, he followed right behind Liz.

"Dad, what time do you think I should pull out," Bill questioned.

"It is four o'clock now, how about in an hour — five p.m."

"Great, that will give me a chance to go see Delta. How about six p.m. — won't that work, Dad? I want to have a little bit more time to see Delta," Bill suggested.

"Not a problem, Son," Dad replied.

Bill jumped into his truck and headed down to Dubbs. The dust was flying behind his truck. In the Mississippi Delta, you can see someone coming because of the flat land so when their vehicle creates so much dust, you sure can see them a long way off.

Delta could feel her heart pounding. Her whole body throbbed to feel Bill's embrace, warm kisses, and sweet voice. There was no way that she was not going to see him. She rushed to her closet, found the fullest dress and quickly slipped into it. She straightened her hair and managed to touch herself up with some powder, blush, and lipstick.

Fortunately for her, Daddy had driven home on the tractor just in time to intercept Bill. She could see from her bedroom window that if she did not step outside, Daddy would unintentionally take away her time with Bill. She did not mind. She knew that Bill and Daddy were friends.

Delta walked out the back door, heading for the backyard. She did not want to appear forward, as Mama would call it. Bill immediately saw her.

"Delta, excuse me, Mr. Earl, but I need to see Delta," he insisted, holding back a run toward her.

"Oh, yes, Bill, you go right ahead. I hope to see you soon. You treat that horse of yours right and you will bring home a ribbon and some money to boot," Earl said.

Bill was halfway to where Delta was standing as Earl was still talking. He certainly prayed that Earl understood. He had missed 'his girl, Delta' for too long.

"Delta," he called out, "I need to see you."

Delta turned around in a southern lady's turn as if to say, "Are you calling me?" All along, she wanted to run just as quickly into his arms; nonetheless, Mama had instilled the importance of being a lady at all times.

Holding Delta very close and lifting her up off the ground, Bill turned her around. At this moment, he gave her a warm kiss. He did not care who was looking.

"You really have been eating your family's garden pickings," he told her as he sat her down.

"Now, now, Bill, that isn't a nice thing to say to a lady," she smiled, even if it was true. "Yes, I just can't seem to get enough of all that is placed on my plate," she confessed.

"Don't you worry your pretty head one minute about that, you will lose every bit of it with everything that has to be done on this farm," he expressed, trying to back-pedal from his original statement.

"Honestly, I was surprised to see you coming," Delta confessed.

"I have to leave tonight for Oxford for a rodeo but I just felt I could not leave without seeing you, Delta. I love you so very much. I have been working out with Cheyenne and the time just slips away," he said.

"Bill," Delta took on more of a serious tone, "when you get a chance for us to have some time alone together, I must talk to you, it is very important. When do you think that might be," she questioned, hoping that it could be soon.

"Delta, I have three back-to-back rodeos scheduled but when I get home from them, you are all mine, every ounce of me. I promise, baby," he replied. By this time, he was gazing directly into her eyes, "Delta, I love you with all I know how to love and I look forward to being with you soon. Please understand that all the words I tell you are what my heart truly feels. I must go for now but I will be home in about three weeks for one of the finest dates this town has ever seen."

Bill headed towards his truck, backed out, and headed toward home.

Tears rolled down Delta's face as she watched his truck drive out of sight. Her heart was hurting. She was wondering where and how she would find the words to let him know she was having a baby and how this baby came to be.

Cheyenne followed close behind Lawrence as they came closer and closer toward the trailer. Bill parked the truck and headed to the barn to help with the loading of Cheyenne. Cheyenne's eyes widened as he saw Bill walking toward him and then he gave out a snicker.

"We are going to do some good riding," Bill said as he gently stroked his mane with one hand and rubbed down his nose with the other. "Okay, Chey, come on into the trailer stall." Without hesitation, he stepped into the stall. "That is great, boy," he stated as he patted him along his side.

"Dad, I am all packed and ready to go. Will you please tell Mom that I love her? I will be looking for all of you guys l," Bill spoke as he turned the key to start the engine.

"You bet, I will, Son. Now, drive safely and keep a lookout for us, Martha Rose and Mary, too, in the stands," Lawrence said as he tapped the side of the door.

Bill was on his way to the Lafayette County Rodeo. He

waved his cowboy hat out the window to his dad and sounded the horn three times, which was a family tradition that stood for good luck.

Life seemed absolutely right for Bill Lawson. It was a beautiful day for some windshield time. With Oxford an eighty-mile drive from home, it was the perfect time for Bill to do some thinking about Delta.

His thoughts went back to the day the two of them drove into town to go on a riverboat cruise. He smiled. The day began with a cloudless sky. For most of the trip, they were talking about Cheyenne and the upcoming rodeo, when Delta noticed a dark cloud which had suddenly formed in the west. They dismissed it as a thunderstorm brewing near a small town just across the Mississippi River; it was certainly nothing for concern. Bill parked the truck and went inside with Delta to purchase the tickets.

Just as they were leaving the building, lightning struck! There were loud roars of thunder and Bill screamed for Delta to run toward the small building where they would normally board the cruise. Then, heavy rain began. As good timing would have it, the two of them just made it inside before the bottom fell out. The sky was totally dark, winds were whipping the small place; they both believed it would vanish at any moment. Bill cushioned her from as much of the deluge as possible. He could not help but think how very special she had become to him. He certainly would protect her as much as he could. There were a lot of people huddled in that little building which stood up to the storm.

As the dark clouds parted, the captain made an announcement that there would still be a cruise on the Mississippi River; it would just take place an hour later. Bill and Delta decided that since they had already gone through so much, they would go on the cruise as planned.

The day that had started in brightness and advanced to middling darkness, now ended in a starry night filled with food, music, dancing, and fun. He could still envision his beautiful brunette looking into his eyes as they slowly danced underneath the moonlit sky; how good it made his heart feel.

Black smoke billowed from the big diesel engine as he backed into the park arena. It was a nice big rig; the trailer behind him must have held six horses. Bill wondered if any of these horses would become his foe tonight.

A guy jumped out of the truck and motioned Bill to come around him. Bill waved as he passed. The guy was dressed as you would expect any deserving cowboy would with blue jeans, a red western shirt, cowboy boots, and a hat.

"Do you only have that one horse?" he yelled out to Bill.

"He can get the job done," Bill shouted back.

Bill dropped down the big gate and whistled for Cheyenne to step out. He pawed one hoof down twice as if giving Bill the okay, and then the big palomino advanced. He was a horse born to show. He had a beautiful silky mane and tail which glistened in the sun. He pulled his head back and gave out a snicker. Bill grinned.

"Showoff," he said, patting him on the neck. They both knew they had come to win.

The arena was packed with people. Bill knew his family would be there and he was really glad of that; the only thing that would make the night complete was if Delta could be there to see him ride.

Tonight, he was competing in calf roping which is also referred to as tie-down roping. Bill and Cheyenne had learned from working on the farm together exactly what to expect from the other. The event has been around since the first rodeo in Cheyenne, Wyoming in 1872. In this event, the cowboy ropes a running calf around the neck with a lariat and his horse stops and sets back on the rope. At the same time, the cowboy dismounts, runs to the calf, throws it to the ground and ties three of its feet together. A well-trained horse will slowly back up while the cowboy ties the calf to help keep the lariat snug.

Bill could feel his blood pumping harder as he heard the noise of the crowd. Liz loved for him to wear his dark jeans, navy cowboy shirt, tan cowboy boots and a tan cowboy hat. She said that it showed him off the best beside the palomino. He hoped she would not be disappointed tonight.

The time had come. Bill and Cheyenne were next. Bill rubbed Cheyenne's mane just as he came down the hall outside the gate, and said, "You show them, Chey."

They were now positioned to start their event. The announcement sounded, "Bill Lawson riding Cheyenne." The calf was released and out behind it they came. Bill could feel his adrenaline flowing. By now, the lariat was around the calf's neck and Cheyenne was slowly backing up keeping the lariat snug. Good Chey, Bill thought. Then he heard his time, 9.4 seconds. By this time the crowd was standing on their feet. Bill felt it was more for Cheyenne than him. But hey, that was all right by him. He leaned over to pick up his hat and there in the middle-left of the crowd sat his family. He smiled and waved his hat.

Then he heard over the loudspeaker that he was the winner. He let out a southern yell! He had taken the first-place prize of $3,000.00. He was happy and could not wait to tell Delta.

He had Cheyenne loaded and was just closing the gate when he heard a voice from behind, "Nice ride out there, Cowboy." He turned around and it was the cowboy who had jumped out of the big rig earlier in the day.

"Thanks, but I could not have done it by myself," Bill replied as he introduced himself.

"Pleased to meet you, Bill. My name is Jerry Bennett. I help the Crawford's out during the rodeos. I don't believe I have ever seen you ride, 'cause I think I would remember that horse," Jerry said.

"I am not able to make every rodeo. I have to help my dad with our farm," Bill answered.

"Where are you from?" Jerry questioned.

"Dundee," he told him.

"Man, I can't believe I do not know you. I live with my family in the Two-Mile-Lake community. But hey, you can't know everybody. I will see you around. I had better get on over to check in with Mr. Crawford," he stated before heading off.

"You bet," Bill said as he jumped in the cab of his truck and headed home.

Chapter Twelve

Jerry Wants a Job

"Cheyenne, boy, you got the job done," Bill spoke as he brushed and stroked the big palomino's hair. "I thought for a while James Turner was going to take the lead but he could not handle what you brought to the arena."

The barn door opened and Lawrence came up to the stall where Bill and Cheyenne were standing.

"We sure are proud of you two. I hate that we could not see you after the show last night but the crowd was just too big to navigate," he said.

"Hey, Dad, don't give it a second thought. We won. I saw you guys in the crowd; just as I reached for my hat, my eyes caught the sight of you. Weren't you proud of Cheyenne? Didn't he pull back just right so I could make the rope hold the calf?" Bill replied.

"You bet. Son. We need to talk. Earlier today a young guy came up to me while I was working in the yard, and said he was Jerry Bennett from the Two-Mile-Lake community. He told me that he met you yesterday. Is this the truth?" Lawrence questioned.

"Yes, I met him at the rodeo. As a matter of fact, I saw him early in the day and then after the event, he came over to me to introduce himself and compliment me on my ride. That is about the extent of it, though," Bill responded.

"Well, it seems he is looking for work; he wondered if we could hire him. He told me that he worked for the Crawford folks but would like something closer to home. He also said that he only worked for them during the rodeo season. What do you think? Do we have enough work around here to justify hiring him so that he would earn a decent paycheck? What do you think of the guy?" he asked.

"Dad, I only just met him. I couldn't say whether he was good or bad. As far as work goes, I guess we could give him about forty hours a week. Sorry, I don't have more to give you but that's it," Bill said as he opened the gate to let Cheyenne out into the pasture.

Lawrence rubbed his hand across his face and then lifted his hat, wiped the sweat from his hair with his handkerchief and replaced his hat. He finally stated, "I'll put a pen to it," and then headed back to the house.

Bill could not wait to see Delta and tell her the news. He headed home to clean up and drive over to see her. It had been too long, as far as he was concerned. The girl was deep in his heart and he knew it.

Just as he entered the kitchen there was his mom. "Hi, Mom," he said as he reached out to hug her. He picked her off the floor and swung her around before kissing her on her forehead.

"Bill, I am so proud of you. Your ride was perfect. We were all so excited," she exclaimed.

"I appreciate that Mom, but Cheyenne deserves a lot of the credit. I'm just a man with a great horse," Bill replied.

"You had better give that some more thought. You know you have taught Cheyenne everything he knows. It takes the both of you to complete the job," she stated emphatically. "Anyway, I am proud of both of you."

"Thanks. Mom, I am anxious to see Delta, so I am going to get a shower and head over to her house. I will see you later tonight," he commented.

"You tell Delta, hello to me. Go right ahead, I know she will be glad to see you and hear your news," she replied as she smiled and winked at him.

Dust was rolling out from behind the truck as it drew closer toward Delta's house. He just could not wait until the next two rodeos were done before seeing her. His heart ached for her. Being around her enriched his life and he would love to make it permanent. However, earning a living was important to him and at the moment, he did not feel he was able to do that.

Mr. Earl greeted him at the door. "Come on in, I heard of that great ride last night. I know you are proud of that horse you have."

"You bet I am, Mr. Earl. Good to see you and thank you for the compliment," Bill responded. "Sir, I came to visit Delta, is she around?"

"No, Bill, Delta and her Mama rode into Tunica for some shopping. I know she will be disappointed that she missed you. Hard to tell when they will return. You know women and shopping; they go together. You are welcome to wait if you want to do so."

"I appreciate that, sir, but I guess I will head back to the farm for there is a lot of work that needs doing. By the way, Mr. Earl, you have been around this part of the county most of your life, so I have a question for you. Dad is considering hiring a new guy, Jerry Bennett. Anything you can tell me about what kind of man he is," Bill asked.

The question stopped Earl in his tracks. What in the world would he say? As far as he knew, no one but the Bennett family and Sheriff Miller had any knowledge of what had taken place. "Honestly, Bill, the Bennett folks have never been known around here as reliable. Well, doggone it, I may as well tell you how I feel. I just do not care for the man. The decision as to whether to hire him or not will have to be up to your family," Earl replied.

"I appreciate your honesty, sir; I will pass it along to Dad. I had better get home. It was good to see you; and please tell Delta I stopped by," Bill spoke as he headed out of the door.

"You bet, Son, I will be happy to let her know. She will be disappointed in missing your visit. Come again, any time for you know you are welcome," Earl stated.

He walked back to his chair with a world of troubles on his mind. He was in a quandary as to tell Delta or just let her find it out for herself. In the past, she had not been around the Lawson farm. He just did not like keeping things from her. He had not seen nor heard from the Bennett bunch since their last encounter and that was the way he liked it. Delta lived through a day from hell; just the thought of that bunch made him cuss. They could go straight to hell as far as he was concerned.

Bill hung his hat on the hat rake as he called out, "Is anyone home?"

"We are all in the den, Son. Come in and join us," Liz said. "How was Delta?" she immediately questioned.

"Sorry, Mom, my lady was not at home. Delta and her mama drove into Tunica to shop. Mr. Earl invited me to wait but I thought I had better get back home. I do hate that I missed seeing her. Maybe it is just as well. She has something that she wants to talk to me about and tonight probably was not the best time. I am going to run out and check on Cheyenne. I won't be long," Bill said.

He stepped outside. It was a beautiful night. Life seemed so perfect to him. He whistled for Cheyenne and within seconds he stepped up. He stroked his silky mane. He knew God had blessed him with one special horse. Cheyenne pulled up his right leg and tapped the ground twice.

"What's on your mind? We have another rodeo the day after tomorrow and we have to be ready," he spoke as he placed the saddle across his back. If he could not be with Delta, at least he could have a good time with Cheyenne. He began his ride.

Lawrence gave Jerry a call to let him know that he could give him a job but he would be on a ninety-day trial.

"Thank you, Mr. Lawson, you won't regret it," Jerry replied.

Jerry was put to work digging fence post holes out in the western part of the farm. This was hard work and his concentration was intense for he never heard the horse approaching until the shadow fell across the ground. He stopped working, leaned against the post hole digger, and pushed his hat back in order to see the rider.

"Hi, Jerry looks like Dad has given you a hard job right off the bat," Bill said.

Jerry took the handkerchief from his back pocket and wiped the sweat from his face before speaking. "Yep, guess this is the hardest work I have done in quite a while. Although, I am not complaining about it because I'm glad to earn some money."

Bill took his canteen from the saddle and offered Jerry a

drink. "Guess you could use some water now," Bill said, holding the canteen in his direction.

"Thanks, but I have a bucket over in the shade. I'll get some here in a minute. Where are you headed?" Jerry questioned.

"Cheyenne and I need to break out some cattle from over the ridge and get them back into the pasture. Anyway, we need a workout to keep in shape for the rodeo coming up," Bill responded.

"You do have one fine horse to ride. Where did you get him?" Jerry asked.

"Bred right here on this farm from Lone Wolf and a mare named Silhouette. He is the best horse I have ever ridden and money could not buy him," Bill answered, smiled, and rode away. He figured he had kept Jerry from work long enough.

That guy has got everything, Jerry thought as he jammed the digger back into the hard dirt. He wondered how many women he had gotten laid. Probably plenty, was his thought. He certainly never had to force any of them but bet he has never had as good as what I have gotten, even if I did have to take it!

Damn, I can't even brag about it. I got away with something that some men are spending time in jail for doing; best I get this off my mind. I hate those sons-a-bitches, anyway, got it all and they know it, fancy trucks, cars, horses, and women. Look at me out here sweating and digging holes for a living while he rides his ass off on a fine horse, really not doing any kind of work. Jackass! I could hit him where it hurts if I mind too.

"Dad, I can't put my finger on it but I think there is something to what Mr. Earl said about Jerry Bennett. Do you truly trust him because I sure don't?" he asked.

Lawrence shook his head. "Maybe I should have put a little more thought into it. You watch him and if you see anything that he has done wrong, let me know."

Bill added, "One thing he smells awful all the time. Do you think the guy ever bathes?"

"I'll be damned if I know, Son," Lawrence laughed out loud.

Several weeks passed and Bill was keeping a watchful eye on Jerry. It was about two thirty in the afternoon when Bill walked into the barn and saw Jerry lingering around Cheyenne.

"Man, what are you up to?" Bill questioned as he walked inside the stall. "You get this straight, nobody, and I mean nobody, touches this horse, especially you! I don't want to catch you anywhere near Chey. You got it?"

"Damn, man, don't get so touchy. I was just looking at the damn horse. What do you think I was doing?" Jerry replied with little fear in his voice. He was a Bennett and he didn't like being talked to in this manner. He pushed his hat back and moved toward Bill.

"Come on, you want some of this, I will be happy to give it to you," Jerry spoke, drawing back his fist. "Man, I could whoop your ass before you would know what had happened to you," he said, grabbing Bill by the collar of his shirt.

"Take your filthy hands off of me, you crazy man," Bill yelled, drawing his fist back and hitting him in the stomach. "Get the hell off this farm and don't show your face around here again. You got it!" he concluded.

Jerry stood up and picked his hat up from off the ground. "You have not heard the last of me, son-of-a-bitch; you can take that to the bank. You rich guys think you own the world," Jerry shouted as he headed out of the barn to his truck.

Bill straightened his shirt and stoked Cheyenne in an effort to cool off. Guess it is time I had better go tell Dad what just happened he thought as he closed the stall door.

Chapter Thirteen

Cheyenne Wins Washington County Rodeo

Most rodeo days began the same. I always take Cheyenne out to loosen him up and get us used to working together. He is such a fine specimen of a horse. He has an inbred ability to work cattle and is able to produce quick bursts of speed. He has an uncanny ability to adjust to the different challenges each calf represents and he must be able to do all of that on his own. Cheyenne has all of these strengths and then some. I am so very proud to own him. When we are working together, it is always difficult to find another team that can beat us. He is smart; he knows how I use the reins to correct him and with the equipment we work with, he can anticipate my every command. When I am precise, Cheyenne will be precise. He watches the calf so that it has no edge on him. He watches my actions and steadfastly holds the rope tight, so the calf cannot move. I give Cheyenne plenty of praise for he deserves it.

"Bill," Dad calls out.

"I am out here, Dad, working with Cheyenne,"

"We will not be at the rodeo tonight, Son. I hope you understand. Your mother is a bit under the weather; it will be best if she stays in bed," Dad informs Bill.

"Sure, I understand, Dad. I will miss you but I will give

you a report when I return home. I wish I had time to go visit Delta but I just don't see how time will allow for it. If you happen to see her, please let her know that I will be thinking about her and that I will for sure be by after this rodeo.

"Greenville is quite a drive, especially when you are pulling a horse trailer, so I guess I had better get started," Bill said as he stepped into the cab of the truck. He gave his usual cowboy wave and three blasts of the horn.

Bill could not help but think of Delta and he knew that she had to be wondering why he had not been to see her. Lately, it just seemed to be one thing and then another but things would get better was his thinking. Little did he know what difficulties were ahead of him.

He was assigned to stall #26. After getting Cheyenne settled, he wanted to spend some time giving him a good brush down. He knew how much he liked that. "Cheyenne, we are going to win this thing. I know I can count on you, now you just count on me," he said as he stroked his mane and prepared it for the show. As he looked to the side of him, some boots came into view that were very familiar, for they were dirty boots as always.

"Jerry, why are you here?" he questioned.

"Well, I thought I would drop by to wish you and that fine horse you have good luck," he said with a smirk.

"I don't need your good wishes so just go on back from where you came," Bill pointed as he looked him directly in the eyes.

"Okay, old boy, I will see you around," Jerry replied and then headed around to the arena.

The Washington County arena was full to the brim. It usually was. Bill and Cheyenne were ready. All they needed was to hear their name called and they would hit the ground running. Bill was not being cocky for he knew he had some strong contenders to bet. There was Jesse Owens and Larry Turner and these were just the two that came to mind. However, he had all the confidence that he and Cheyenne were prepared and ready to take them on.

The gate swung open and they walked toward the entryway. He could hear the announcer loud and clear.

"Folks, get ready for Bill Lawson is next at the gate and he is riding the magnificent horse, Cheyenne. We are all in for what I believe is a superb ride. All of you give it up for Bill Lawson," the announcer concluded in his introduction. The crowd was on their feet with anticipation.

Bill could, as always, feel the adrenaline pumping because he knows timing is critical. He knows he must have Cheyenne at a gallop from the box shortly after the calf leaves the chute. Valuable time is saved by Cheyenne being at nearly full speed the moment the barrier releases.

They are off; the barrier releases and outran a black calf. Cheyenne is at top speed and Bill, swinging his lariat to lasso the calf, signaled Cheyenne to stop quickly while he dismounts and runs to the calf. He gets to the calf, wrestles it to the ground and flips it onto its side; then he ties three of the calf's legs together using a half hitch knot, or as it is sometimes referred to as a 'wrap and a slap'. The big palomino is trained to assist Bill by slowly backing away from the calf to maintain a steady tension on the rope.

Once the tie is complete, Bill throws his hands in the air to signal 'time' to stop the clock. He returned to mount Cheyenne and moved him forward to relax the tension on the rope. The calf must stay tied five seconds before an official time is recorded.

Then he heard his time echoing over the loudspeaker… 7 seconds. Best time recorded ever at the Washington County Rodeo. The crowd erupts.

Bill was bursting inside with pride not for himself, but for Cheyenne. He had trained Cheyenne to bend one foot and take a bow. On cue, the big palomino bowed for the crowd. Everyone was on their feet. What a show! Bill was experiencing a high adrenaline rush felt on top of the world. He would carry home a $6,000.00 prize for the ride.

Little did he realize that there, in the confines of the arena, a man full of hate and resentment was an explosion waiting to happen. Jerry looked through the opening onto the arena floor and thought, I hate that son-of-a-bitch. He thinks he has got it all and right now that may be the case but things can change with a single disturbance.

All the way home Bill thought about telling Delta the wonderful news. He certainly did not want to come across as arrogant because he knew that arrogance comes before a fall, but he knew that the work he and Cheyenne had put in earned this win.

On the way home, he stopped to enjoy a juicy steak but it did not take long because he could not wait to get home, tell the family, and plan for the next day when he would go to visit Delta.

He thought that he had better check in with Mr. Earl to see if they were going to be around home and if it would be a good time. So, he stopped in a small town, Shaw, Mississippi to use a payphone to make the call.

Sure enough, Mr. Earl answered the phone and he knew Bill's voice right off the bat. "Hi, Bill, how was the ride?" Mr.

Earl was bursting to know.

"Oh, sir, if you promise not to tell Delta I will fill you in with all of the details. It was a great crowd at the rodeo as it always is and Cheyenne could not have performed any better. We took the grand prize money for calf-roping. If I did not know any better, I believe Cheyenne knew what has just taken place. He could not have done a better job. Mr. Earl, this is no brag, just fact, I have the best horse in the whole wide world," Bill spoke nonstop.

"Congratulations, man, you deserve it and your secret is safe with me. We will be looking forward to your visit tomorrow. Now you drive safely."

"Bye, sir," Bill said as he heard the click of the phone when it disconnected.

He pulled into the long driveway toward the house. The family did not know exactly what time to expect him but he knew they would have been anxious to hear all about the event. He was right.

Mary saw him as the truck and horse trailer turned into the drive and she began to scream, "Bill is home, come on everyone; let's greet him as he drives up."

All of them flooded out of the door and Bill jumped out the cab of the truck, running immediately to Liz. He picked her up and swung her around. From all of his excitement, they knew something grand had taken place.

"Family, are you ready for this?" Bill asked, setting up the moment... "Cheyenne and I took first place and brought home $6,000.00 for the job." By now, he had been around each of the family members for hugs.

"I know Cheyenne is tired of being in that trailer so let me go take care of him. I will rejoin you in the house, clean up a bit and then we can have some supper. I am starving for some of Mama's cooking," he spoke before remembering that she was sick when he left. "Oh, Mama, I am sorry I forgot you have been sick. Hey, I can take us into town for supper. Let's do that because it will be better. Everyone can order what they want and no one will have to do any washing of dishes afterwards."

Liz was still recovering from her virus so that was sweet music to her ears. They all headed into the house to get prepared for the outing while Bill took care of Cheyenne.

Bill came out looking sharp in his Western shirt, blue jeans, snakeskin cowboy boots and cowboy hat. He began the conversation, "You folks ready for some good eating at the Blue & White Café." He knew that was the family's favorite restaurant to eat and there would be no disagreement about that choice. "Why don't we all take in a drive-in movie while we are celebrating?" he interjected.

Of course, the two girls were jumping up and down with excitement. "Oh, Mama, that is if you are up to it?" Bill quickly questioned.

"Sure, Son, I would love that, so we had better get going if we are going to be on time for all of this," Liz said as she gathered her purse and shawl.

One of the favorite meals for the Lawson family is fried catfish and fried catfish just doesn't get any better than when it is served at the Blue & White Café. Sure enough, everyone ordered catfish. The rodeo was discussed at length and everyone was beaming from the delight of such a success. Bill could not say enough good things about Cheyenne. "He is the horse of all horses but I have raised him from the moment his

127

feet touched this earth, so how could he not know the way I think" was Bill's conclusion.

The movie was an enjoyable one for the family, it was *El Dorado,* starring John Wayne. The movie was about Cole Thornton, a gunfighter for hire, who joins forces with an old friend, Sheriff J.P. Hara. Together, with an old Indian fighter and a gambler, they help a rancher and his family fight a rival rancher who is trying to steal their water.

John Wayne had starred in some great movies, *Rio Bravo* in 1959 and *The Man Who Shot Liberty Valance* in 1962, so any opportunity to catch one of his films was a treat.

Chapter Fourteen

Bill's Heart is Broken

Yesterday evening had been such an enjoyable one for the Lawson family but today was a new day and a lot of things needed attention on the farm.

Lawrence finished his breakfast, headed out to the back porch, placed his cap on his head and started for the barn to check on the animals. This event took place pretty much in the same manner every morning. Thoughts were running through his head, Bill must really be worn out because he is usually up by this time and on hand to go with him. However, Lawrence understood that rodeos take a lot out of a person, and so did all of the celebrating they had done last night.

Everything appeared in order with most of the farm critters. He had some baby piglets that were growing like weeds and it was a mighty good thing to see. He walked over to the horse stalls to see how their night had gone. All of the Quarter Horses were looking forward to some sweet feed so he brought the bucket with him fully well knowing this would be the case. He began at stall one and went down the line. As he reached Cheyenne's stall, he could see that he was not standing. What in the world is going on, Lawrence thought?

Oh, my goodness, he is down. The stall door could not open fast enough for Lawrence. Landing on his knees he reached trying to find the big palomino's pulse but it was faint, if at all.

He rushed back to the house and used the first telephone he came to, which was in the kitchen, to call Vet Carter. As Vet Carter answered the phone, he explained the situation.

"I will be right there, Vet Carter told him, in the meantime, place a blanket over him. I am on my way."

Thank goodness the family was in some other part of the house because he did not have time to do any explaining. He rushed back to the barn and did as the vet had instructed with a prayer in his heart that something could be done.

Vet Carter arrived and went straight to the barn. He checked Cheyenne from head to toe. "Lawrence, I have some bad news. This horse has experienced an air embolism," he said as he looked into the confused eyes of the farmer.

"What is that?" questioned Lawrence.

"Someone has injected air into an artery. That's what it means," the vet explained.

Lawrence staggers back to the side of the stall, takes off his hat, and begins to cry. Taking his handkerchief from his pocket he blew his nose. After clearing his throat, he once again tried to ask the question that was hard to put into words. "Will he live?" he asked.

"I am sorry, Lawrence, but there is nothing that can save this valuable animal's life. This was an intentional act," stated Vet Carter.

Lawrence turned red in the face. "I bet I know exactly who is guilty of this… Jerry Bennett would be who I suspect."

"Well, if I were you, I would place a call to the sheriff's office just to see what is to be done from here," and with those words, they both heard Cheyenne draw his last breath.

Lawrence wept and the vet did his best to console him but Lawrence knew the hardest part was yet to come… telling Bill. With the vet's job done, he left Lawrence to this great insurmountable task.

Lawrence picked up another blanket, spreading it over Cheyenne's head as tears flowed from his eyes and dropped onto the blanket. He stands, closes the stall door and heads toward the house.

He could hear laughter as he came closer toward the house. By this time, all of the family was in the kitchen sharing their thoughts about the movie and how funny it was when Mary tripped on the steps going into the Blue & White.

Lawrence dreaded opening the door. The door slammed behind him. He knew it would be an impossible task for them not to see the anguish in his face but it could not be helped for there was no way to change it; this is what pain like this does. Now it was his task to inflict this same feeling onto his son. Only, to his son, the pain would be so much greater, for Cheyenne was so much more than an animal. He was a member of the family.

He takes his hat off, hangs it on the holder and walks into the kitchen.

Liz noticed it first. "Lawrence, what is wrong? Are you sick? Please come sit down for I am afraid you might just faint," Liz spoke, holding on to his broad shoulders and leading him to the chair. By this time, Bill was on the other side of his father.

"No, Liz, I am not sick, at least not in the way you mean." He struggled to get the words out without bursting into tears.

"Dad, I can't remember when, if ever I have seen you like this," Bill said as he bent down on one knee to try to look into

131

his father's eyes.

"Son, family, it is Cheyenne, it is Cheyenne. He is dead," Lawrence said and burst into tears, grabbing hold of his son.

"Did I just hear you right, Dad?" Bill said as he stood and walked back toward the door. Then he turned in confusion and ran back to his dad.

By this time, Lawrence was standing. "This cannot be some kind of a joke for it would not be funny at all," Bill spoke, grasping for words to make some sense of this situation.

"I'm so very sorry, Son." Lawrence grabbed hold of Bill to look at him directly in the eyes. "I wish it were not so and I wish I could change it, but I cannot. I called Vet Carter and he came immediately. He told me that there was nothing that could be done because Cheyenne had been injected with air into his artery. He and I heard him when he drew his last breath."

"Injected, who in the world would do something like that?" Bill questioned. Without hearing the answer, Bill ran to the barn.

There, lay his beautiful Cheyenne. He fell to his knees weeping and lay by the still-warm animal's side. He pulled the blanket back from his face trying to see life in those golden eyes but they were still and unconscious. He rubbed his beautiful mane as he had so many times before and wished for him to stand up. His eyes were swelling from all of the painful tears that had fallen from them. He thought of all the pleasure Cheyenne had brought to him and hoped that he had done the same for him.

Bill walked out of the barn into the sunlight. He looked heavenwards and questioned God as to why this was allowed to happen. How could anyone be so cruel? But he knew the devilish man that could do just such a thing and his name was Jerry Bennett. Of course, God did not allow it and he knew that.

I will never saddle Cheyenne any more for our morning ride. Then there were the hundreds of rodeo fans who had come to know Cheyenne and saw the work that he did in the arena; they, too, will miss him. I believe Cheyenne could hold his own with the best of them. He understood me and I understood him. How could Cheyenne not understand? I had ridden and trained him since he pulled himself up on his small legs and took his first steps. We bonded instantaneously. He knew what I wanted and expected of him. Tears dropped to the ground.

After giving Bill a respectable time to say goodbye, Liz and Lawrence went to where Bill sat in the pasture. "Son, we are so sorry for this great pain that you are having to journey through. Please know that we are here, if only to be a shoulder to cry on or someone to talk with during the coming days," Liz softly spoke.

Lawrence hated to bring up such a delicate subject but he had to know where and what to do with the body. "Son, we have to discuss what you want to do about Cheyenne's body," he respectfully urged.

Bill thought for a minute. "Dad, there is a ridge that he and I worked out on so many times. Do you mind if we have his body placed there?" Bill questioned.

Without hesitation, Lawrence told him that would be fine by him. "I will go now to make the arrangements. Folks, will please excuse me," Lawrence said and then headed back to the house.

After saying goodbye, Lawrence drove to the local lumber

company. There he purchased eighty boards made of oak. He figured this amount through the size and weight of Cheyenne. He instructed the craftsman exactly how he wanted them cut. Of course, this coffin would look quite different from one made for a human.

Lawrence spotted a payphone on his way to the store, so while the craftsman was cutting the boards, he excused himself to make a call. He knew of a local man that had a small excavator that he felt certain he could borrow to lift the coffin into the ground. He explained the situation and Glen had no problem helping him out.

"It appears I have perfect timing," Lawrence spoke to the man cutting the boards. The man gave a nod and continued finishing the job.

On the drive home, his thoughts were of Bill. There are no words that could lessen the pain but he would do his best to design and construct a burial coffin for Cheyenne.

He worked late into the night until he had only one last thing to add. Liz had given him a quilt that she had made some years back. He placed it securely inside the box. It fit as if it had been made for that very purpose. With the last nail being placed, he closed the lid.

It was a sunny Friday morning when the family all gathered on the ridge on the west side of the farm. The box was lowered into the soft earth where it was placed. It was a solemn time for the family for they all knew the depth of pain being felt in this one man's heart. Each of the family took a flower and placed it on the ground; then each filed away by giving Bill a hug to say I love you, leaving him some private time to say farewell to his beloved Cheyenne.

There, on the ridge, Bill placed a white wooden tombstone

that read:

"Cheyenne"
Born: May 3, 1960
Died: August 24, 1965
Gave all he had to give;
Bill's praise & joy!

Chapter Fifteen

Will There Be Justice for Cheyenne?

Lawrence realized that Bill, due to his grieving, had not truly understood what was said about the killing of Cheyenne. He went to Liz to discuss it with her.

"Liz, I know that I have got to bring the killing of Cheyenne back to Bill's attention because we need to go see Sheriff Miller. When do you think I should do this?" he asked.

"Lawrence, right now there is no good time. I think you need to bring it to his attention so that it can be looked into. It is not that we will truly ever know who did this horrible thing but at least we should try," she answered.

"I will talk to him today when he returns from town. Do you know if he has seen Delta recently?" Lawrence asked.

"I am not aware of any visits he has made to Delta. He has not mentioned it to me but he does not tell me everything," Liz replied.

It was not until late afternoon when Bill returned home. Lawrence could not have dreaded anything anymore but it had to be discussed.

Bill walked into the house, placed his hat on the rack and called out, "Is anyone home?

"Bill," Lawrence said, "could you please come into my study for we need to talk?"

"Yes, sir, let me grab a glass of tea. Would you like one?" he asked.

"No, I appreciate the offer, though," Lawrence told him.

"I am so appreciative of you and Mom. I have had a rough day. How about all of you?" he asked.

"Please close the door," Lawrence instructed him.

Bill did as he was told.

"This sounds like something serious, Dad. Do we need Mom in here?" Bill asked.

Lawrence spoke, "Well, yes, it is serious, but your mom is aware of what I will be talking to you about. A lot has taken place in the last week. I told you that Cheyenne was intentionally killed by someone injecting air into his artery. Vet Carter advised that we discuss this with the sheriff." He gave it time to register with Bill.

"Son of a gun, Dad, I can tell you exactly the person responsible for this... It is Jerry Bennett," he spoke as he walked toward the window.

"I agree with you but proving it is another thing. We need to go immediately to see Sheriff Miller," Lawrence emphatically said.

"Let's go do this thing, Dad. Are you ready?" Bill was looking directly at his dad as he spoke.

"I'm ready. Let's just let your mom know that we will be leaving and then we will head out."

They wasted no time reaching town and the sheriff's office. It was about six p.m. Luckily, the sheriff was there, and available.

"Sheriff, I know you are familiar with the Bennett family, including all of the sons," Lawrence spoke first.

"Yep, a little more than I would like to be," replied the

sheriff.

Bill was pacing the floor as all was being said but holding back to let his dad do the talking.

"We experienced a tragic event at our farm. Cheyenne, Bill's prize horse, was killed. Intentionally, I might add. Vet Carter said he was injected with air in an artery. He called it by some medical name. I don't remember, but he can tell you." Lawrence pushed his chair back from the table, leaned back on it, and waited for the sheriff's response.

Sheriff Miller drops his head. He was biting his lower lip. "You think Jerry Bennett is responsible? If so, where is your proof?" the sheriff questioned.

By this time, Bill could stand it no longer and he began to speak. "Sheriff, he hates my guts, not that I know for sure why but I know he does. He worked out at the farm for a while. I caught him hanging around Cheyenne and I made him understand never to come around again, nor around Cheyenne, period. We got into a fight because he grabbed me by the collar and I told him to get off our farm, never to come back," Bill told the sheriff. "Now, I want to know what you are thinking?" he questioned.

"Listen, guys, I understand and I am very sorry for your loss, but these kinds of things are so very hard to prove. I will talk with Vet Carter and then visit the Bennett family to talk to them. That is all I can promise at this point. Do you understand? Please do not try to take things into your own hands. Let the law handle this," Sheriff Miller concluded.

"Thank you, Sheriff, we appreciate it. We will of course abide by the law," Lawrence said. He turns to look into Bill's eyes. He could see the anguish but he felt helpless to do anything about it.

"Son, please know how I hurt for you because I know how much Cheyenne meant to you, but we must take this thing a day at a time. God will comfort us through this. This is what we must rely on and believe," Lawrence said as he hugged his son tightly.

They both walked out of the sheriff's office. Lawrence remembered that he needed to pick up some sweet feed for the horses, so he headed toward the Tunica County Co-Op. Bill followed along mainly because he did not want to be alone.

"Gosh dang it, Dad, with all the things that have been happening, I have not talked to Delta. I guess she thinks I don't care anymore." When we got back home, I plan on going over to see her, he decided.

It did not take long at the feed store before they were headed for home. Bill helped his dad put all of the farm products in the barn.

"Dad, I am going to go inside and get ready to go see Delta, if that is okay with you?" he said.

"No, Son, I do not mind. You go. Thank you for all of the help today and drive carefully. I will see you later," Lawrence replied.

It did not take Bill long to get ready. He said his goodbyes to his family and started on his way to see Delta.

As he drove alone, he wondered what she had been up to these days for it seemed like forever since he had seen her. Could she possibly know of his loss of Cheyenne? News travels fast in these parts, so he would have to believe she had heard by now. But why had she not gotten in touch with him?

When he drove up, Mr. Earl was out in the yard and, as always, he was glad to see him.

"Howdy, Mr. Earl, how have you been?" Bill said as he

reached out his hand.

"Oh, I can't complain. I have been working hard in the fields but that is nothing new. I was truly sorry to hear of the death of your horse. I know that you loved that horse like family. If there is anything that I can do to help you, I hope you will let me know," Earl told him.

"I appreciate that, sir. It was a hard thing for me and my family to go through, especially since we know it was a deliberate act. Of course, we believe we know who did it but proving it is difficult," Bill said.

"Deliberate, you say. Who do you think did it? Do you mind telling me?" Earl asked.

"Jerry Bennett, sir. He worked for us for a short while but his work was not up to standards and I caught him several times hanging around Cheyenne. I told him not to be anywhere near him but he ignored me, so he and I got into a fight and I told him to leave our property and never come back. It was not too many days later that Cheyenne was found killed by an injection of air into an artery, so it does not take too much to put two and two together," replied Bill.

Earl wondered if Bill could see the anger raging inside. Just the mention of Jerry Bennett made his blood boil. He decided it might be best if he tried to change the subject.

"Bet you are here to see Delta? Do you have that right?" he questioned.

"Yes, sir, is she here?" Bill answered.

"She sure is. Just knock on the front door there and one of them will let you inside," Earl said all along knowing that tonight would most likely be a turning point in their relationship. He watched as Bill walked up to the house and his heart ached, for he knew the kind of hurt he was headed into.

Bill knocked on the door and Ms. Pesh told him to come inside.

"It sure is good to see you Ms. Pesh. I am sorry it has been so long since I have been here; with all the rodeos and situations at home, I have been short of time," he said, opening the conversation.

Pesh wiped her hands on her apron and shook hands with Bill. "It is good to see you and I am sorry about your loss. Is there anything I can do?" she asked.

"Oh, I wish there was, Ms. Pesh, but I guess in time things will get better — at least that is what I am told — but thank you. Is Delta here? I really would like to see her," he asked.

Pesh left the room and went back to get Delta. It just so happened that they had been in town that day, so Delta looked really pretty, but by now she was wearing a maternity dress. Pesh knew this was going to be a shock for Bill and she dreaded to see that happen, but it had to happen. Pesh made sure she found things to do outside in order to give the two of them their privacy.

Bill heard the door slam. His heart began to pound with anticipation of seeing her. His eyes widened as Delta walked into the room. What in the world is going on, were his thoughts? Am I dreaming?

"Hi, Bill, it is so good to see you. It has been a while. As you can see a lot has taken place around here. We need to talk. Please sit down, Bill," Delta said as she directed him toward the couch.

Bill's legs were weakened but somehow, he found himself sitting down and looking at a pregnant woman. It was a sight that he could not believe.

"Can I offer you something to drink?" she asked, knowing full well eating or drinking was the last thing on his mind.

"No, thank you. Delta, I am speechless. You need to talk to me. What is going on? Did you get married without so much as a word?" he questioned.

"Bill, you must let me explain and I assure you that it is going to be difficult both for me and for you."

"Go ahead. I am listening," he said, wondering what was to come next.

"Last spring, late spring, Mama, Daddy, and Peggy went to Mavis' house because she was having her baby. I did not want to be a part of seeing all that and I had some things to do around here, so I talked Mama and Daddy into letting me stay here, which turned out to be the biggest mistake of my life. I went to the garden to gather the vegetables and when I came back to the house and went into the kitchen, three young men were standing behind me. I was very frightened. As you can most likely guess without me going through all of the horrific details, they raped me. It was a day like no other. I did all that I could do to talk them out of their plans but there was no stopping them. They did what they had planned to do when they entered our house. They knew I was alone and that no one would be there to stop them, nor even hear my cries. They finally left. I straightened up the house, took a bath and scrubbed until I felt like my skin would bleed; however, what was done was done. I thought that I would take it to the grave with me but as you can see things did not work out like I thought," Delta stopped speaking to give it some time for Bill to register what she had been through.

"Delta, I ask you, for I have a right to know. Who did this to you?" Bill asked.

This was the same question that first came out of Keith's mouth and now Bill. She took a deep breath. She rose from the couch and excused herself to get a glass of water for her mouth was so dry, it felt like cotton.

After she returned to the room, she could tell Bill was so visibly shaken by all this but she must let him know the truth.

She took a drink and then said, "Jerry Bennett, Wayne and a guy named Max were the young men who raped me, and my baby can belong to either of the three."

She looked at Bill as he was turning as pale as a ghost.

"Delta, you have got to excuse me. My stomach feels like it's tied in knots. I need to go to the bathroom because I am going to be sick," he said, but could not wait to be directed to the bathroom. Instead, he ran outside where he vomited until there was nothing left inside him. Now, he did not know what to say to anyone, Delta, Mr. Earl, or Ms. Pesh, so he just got into his truck and drove away.

Tears were streaming down Delta's face as she watched him leave. I didn't even get a chance to let him know how sorry I was to hear of Cheyenne's death. She had to admit to herself that although she knew it would be difficult for Bill to understand, she never imagined that this would be his reaction.

As she closed the door, she knew that her situation was something that Bill just did not want any part of. Although she felt the great pain of loss, she knew she would have the baby.

Was she prepared for all of the misunderstandings from all of the folks she knew and loved? Everybody will just have to conclude as they desire. I know the truth and that is what counts. Daddy and Mama had been her rock. She was still unsure where Keith stood but she knew he cared and was concerned and for that, she was grateful.

Emotions were building inside Delta. She was trying to hold them back, but when she turned and saw Mama, all bets were off. She ran to the best comfort for her anytime and that was into her mama's arms. Mama's apron came in handy for wiping away the tears.

"Mama, please do not let this upset you. They are just plain old men. May God damn them all!" Delta yelled.

Those words coming out of Delta's mouth startled both of them. Delta burst into tears and ran to Mama, holding her tight. "I am so sorry, Mama, I should not have said such a thing. Please forgive me. Bill is a fine man and I know he has a lot on his mind right now with the death of Cheyenne, and then I go and add some more sorrow."

She could not possibly know how furious it made Bill hearing the name Jerry Bennett come from her mouth as one of three men who had raped her. Hatred was definitely what I felt for Jerry, Rage was building inside Bill, for it was his intention that all the swinging dicks pay, but most especially, Jerry Bennett. There were no redeeming qualities for this man. He was pure evil to the core!

Mama knew how hurt her youngest child must be feeling right now so she had a right to lash out. "Daughter, I love you with all my heart. There is nothing to forgive," Mama said as she wiped the tears from her daughter's eyes.

Chapter Sixteen

Bill Is Going to Wyoming

Bill seemed to be on an endless, no destination ride. He was so angry that he wanted to press the gas pedal all the way to the floorboard. However, being the level-headed man that he was, he knew that would only get him a speeding ticket or worse, jail. How could he go home, he wondered? What could I possibly say to my folks? He was just filled with questions but no answers.

And then, his thoughts turned to Delta. I didn't even give her a chance to at least explain, why didn't I? He turned the pickup around and headed back to see Delta. I can't leave this like this. It is not fair to anyone, Delta or me. All kinds of things entered his thought process but no sooner than they entered, he realized he did not know the answer. I am just wasting my time. I just need to wait until I am face to face with the one person who can give me some answers.

As he put the gear shift in park, he reached for his cowboy hat. He wanted some answers; he was not going to leave until he had them. The door was opening even before Bill placed his hand to knock.

"Mr. Earl, sir, it is not my intent to bother you but I have just got to talk to Delta," he said almost in a pleading voice.

"Sure thing, Bill, I believe the two of you have some unfinished business," Earl answered. He motioned for Bill to enter the house. He would find Delta and give them their privacy.

"Pesh, let's take a walk down to the garden and give these two, time to talk," he spoke, all the while pulling on Pesh's arm to lead them out into the yard.

"Why, Earl, Delta has no idea that Bill is here, does she?" Pesh questioned.

"Yes, I told her. She has been crying so she wanted a chance to try and freshen up a bit. Now, Pesh, we will just go on our way," he said while again, trying to get them away from the house.

Delta eased into the doorway. Bill rose to greet her. "Delta, I apologize for just leaving earlier. You see, Jerry and I do not see eye-to-eye on just about anything. I come close to hating the man. To be truthful with you, I hate this man because I believe, Delta, he is going to someday physically hurt or, even worse, murder someone. When I left here, I was feeling so much pain, and, yes, pain for you. So many things have changed for me, mainly because of the wickedness of one man, Jerry Bennett." Bill spoke with a feeling that he may never stop. "Delta, I should not have left the way I did but I just could not believe the words I was hearing, I have got to hear the story, the whole story, from you, please."

Delta hated reliving this event but she knew that Bill deserved to hear it. Delta began her story, "You cannot believe the horrifying rape that happened to me. The family had gone to be with Mavis because her baby was being born. I wanted to stay here. I went to the garden to pick the vegetables and when I returned there were three men in the house. They each

146

raped me, twice.

"I hate to even think about it. However, things could have been worse, they could have killed me. They did tell me that if I told anyone, they would return and kill us all and I believed they were just that mean. As you can see, I lived through it but as a result of the rape, I am having one of the men's baby." Delta felt her face reddening with shame, not for having the baby, but because just hearing the words brought back floods of memories.

Bill was almost speechless but he had to get the words out of his mouth, "Delta, I hate that this terrible thing happened to you but I am sorry, there is no way that I could ever love this baby. Do you not realize that it could be Jerry Bennett's baby?"

By this time Delta was standing. Her words were carefully chosen, "Yes, Bill, I do know this; but it does not change my love for my baby. I understand your feeling and since this is the way you feel, I know there is no future for us. If you would not mind, I would like you to leave. I need to be alone."

Bill heard the door close behind him. He knew that he loved Delta but life as they knew it had changed. He headed home. This time he could make better life decisions. He had the truth from Delta. He did not plan on telling the family anything about this event. It was no one's business.

He hung his hat on the knob as he had done for years. He stopped before turning the doorknob. The family will just have to believe that because of the killing of Cheyenne, I am headed in a different direction.

"Hey, is anybody home?" Bill called out.

Lawrence folded his paper and said, "Yes, Son, I am here in the living room. Come on in. I am anxious to hear what is going on with you. We have not actually seen you for a few days. Seems you come in late, go to bed and leave before breakfast."

"That just about sums it up, Dad, Bill began to speak. You see, I have been experiencing some pretty dark thoughts. Dad, I could just kill Jerry for what he has done. I believe that if I don't leave, quite possibly I might do just that and then where would I be. I am making plans to go out west to Wyoming. I have spoken to a rancher friend of mine that will put me up and put me to work. I do not think it will be forever but I must put some distance between Jerry and me."

Lawrence could understand Bill's reasoning but it would not make it any easier for the family. Bill had always been loved by all of the family members who were both not so far and far off. It was not long before Liz entered the room.

"Liz, Bill has some news that he wants to share with you. I have already been informed," Lawrence said with a definite sadness in his voice.

The first thing out of Liz's mouth was, "Why don't we have a sandwich?" She could never imagine what was coming up. She just thought it was something that had to do with the farm or maybe he wanted to plan on breeding the two horses with the hope of another Cheyenne.

"Mom," Bill spoke, all the while holding her hand, "I am making plans to move to Wyoming. I need a new direction and a friend of mine has a ranch. I want to go there, not forever, just to get away and clear my mind. I am afraid something bad is going to happen if I stay here."

Liz burst into tears. How could she not see and be with her only son?

"Please, Mom, try to understand this thing from where I stand. I have never looked for trouble but this son-of-a-bitch,

Jerry Bennett, has put it right in front of me. How do I just forget what he did to my Cheyenne? Sheriff Miller does not give me much of a percentage of this guy paying for what he has done. He seems to be a master at getting away with things. Oh, I am not going into anything else that I know. I just know what he did to Cheyenne is enough for me. I do not want to go to jail for killing this guy but Mom, I believe if I run upon him somewhere, I just might do that. Maybe during this time, this guy will move on. I definitely believe that it is the best thing for me."

How could Liz disagree with that? She could not.

"Bill, how soon are you planning on leaving?" Liz asked through tears.

"Soon, Mom, soon," was all Bill could say.

The next few days were utilized helping his dad catch up on things that needed immediate attention on the farm. He would also work with his dad on hiring someone at least part-time because, with Bill gone, his dad would be overloaded.

After that was completed, the family was making plans to go to their favorite restaurant, The Blue & White. This would be their time of good fellowship, eating, and saying their goodbyes. It was not an easy thing to leave the comfort of his family, the farm, friends, and all that he knew. However, he had to face facts that only a few months ago were not there and going out west would be the best option right now.

Chapter Seventeen

The Daze Family Faces Trauma

Delta's baby was getting bigger for even the maternity clothes that one of Peggy's friends, Linida, loaned her were getting tight.

Feeling the need for some fresh air, Delta walked out into the warm summer day. There was a nice breeze blowing but it was still warm. She loved everything about this place. The house had always been the perfect size for their family. It was such a joy to saddle Queen and go for a ride. There were always special places for them to go, even if it was just a ride around the pasture that was close to home.

Suddenly, she heard a noise coming from the barn. It was Queen. Delta quickly ran to see what the commotion was all about. She could see as she came closer to the barn that Daddy was laying on the ground. Queen was close by. She could see that there was blood running down Daddy's face and that he was not moving.

"Daddy, oh, Daddy please speak to me," she yells as she reaches to comfort him.

Unfortunately, he was not making a sound. She tore the end of her dress and wiped the blood that was flowing into his eye.

Delta was not aware but Keith was pulling into their

driveway. He noticed that there was someone out at the barn; it was Delta.

"Delta, are you here?" Keith called out.

"Come quick, Keith. Daddy has been hurt and we need to help him."

Keith could see that immediate attention was needed for Earl. "Delta, I am going to go inside to call an ambulance," he told her, all the while leaving for the house.

Just as he came closer to the house, he thought about not upsetting Mama Pesh but how would he do that, he wondered. Fortunately for him, she was nowhere close by. He reached for the kitchen phone to call for help. He knew Sheriff Miller's office number, so he would leave it to the sheriff to call the ambulance. Keith reached into the kitchen drawer for a towel. It was clean and they would just have to replace it he thought as he hurried out the door.

"Help will be here soon, Delta," he spoke as he looked into her tearful eyes.

"Keith, is my Daddy going to be okay?" she questioned knowing he did not know.

"I talked to Sheriff Miller and help is on the way. Pesh was not in the kitchen but I know she will hear the ambulance. So, Delta, I think it will be best if I go inside to try to brace her for what is coming," he said. She quickly agreed with him.

Arriving back in the kitchen Keith called out to Pesh. She was sewing in the living room. Keith was trying to remain calm believing that if he remains calm, it would help as he explained the situation to her.

She greeted Keith with a hug and smile as she always does.

"Mama Pesh, would you mind if we sit down because I

need to talk with you," he said, trying his best to stay as calm as he possibly could under the circumstances. She looked a bit confused but without hesitation, did as Keith asked her to do.

"Pesh, there has been an accident. It appears that Earl has somehow, we just do not know how, been hurt. Delta is taking care of him until the ambulance gets here. Now, I called for the ambulance because I would believe it best to leave it to medical folks to attend to this kind of thing," Keith said, holding Mama Pesh's hand. He could tell by the look into her eyes that she was doing her best to absorb what she had just been told and then, she broke into tears.

"Keith, please can you help me out there to comfort him?" she asked. He gently helped her stand and they walked out the back door.

Immediately, upon seeing her Mama, Delta ran to her. "Mama, Daddy is going to be okay. We have help coming and, and I just know they will get him better," she said as she held her Mama close.

Sadly, all this time Earl had not made a sound. Pesh could not sit down beside him but she lifted his hand to hold. It was warm and that was good, she thought.

"Listen, ya'll, I hear the siren," Pesh spoke and no sooner than she spoke the words, the medical people were there.

Pesh, Delta, and Keith quickly moved out of their way. It seemed like only minutes before they had Earl on the stretcher and were loading him in the ambulance.

"Delta, you need to go change your dress and I need to gather a few things and we can be on our way to the hospital. Keith, will you please drive us?" Pesh asked, knowing that he would have it no other way.

It seemed like no time before they were pulling onto the

hospital parking lot. They all hurried inside. Of course, they were told to wait, so they waited. Time seemed to move too slowly. Pesh was not the pushy type so Keith decided to approach one of the nurses for answers.

"It will be up to the doctor to speak with you about Mr. Daze," she spoke quietly, "but I can tell you this, Mr. Daze is in surgery."

"Surgery?" Delta could not help but respond. "Why? Will he be okay? I need to know," she pleaded.

"The doctor will be here as quickly as humanly possible," she explained and left for the nurse's area.

Keith did his best to comfort them but he knew that they must be feeling so very frightened. "Ya'll, right now the best thing that we can do is pray for Earl," he said as he reached for both of their hands.

Delta had to talk to Mama about contacting Peggy. She was so far away at college, nonetheless, she must be told of Daddy's condition.

"Mama, I have been giving it some thought about Peggy, You know she will want to know about Daddy?" she asked.

"Yes, Peggy needs to be told. Delta, I am going to leave it up to you to find out how to reach her, for I do not know. You can do that when we get home. I have a copy of her papers and they must contain a phone number where she can be reached," Mama said.

Although they had been there only a few hours, it seemed like days.

"Mama, please let me go get you something to eat. You need to keep up your strength for Daddy," Delta advised.

"I know you mean well but I will be all right. I am just not hungry. I feel like there is something more I can do. Delta, if

153

you can find me a cup of coffee, black please, I would like that." Pesh replied. Upon that request, Delta left to see where some coffee would be in this place.

No sooner than Delta had returned with the coffee, the doctor approached them. "I know you are very concerned about Earl and I will share with you what we know and the procedures that have been done to help him. A head injury is any sort of injury to your brain, skull, or scalp. In Earl's case, it is an injury to his linear skull fracture. In a linear fracture, there is a break in the bone but the bone does not move. Although we are not sure what happened, what we do know is whatever it was has resulted in the loss of consciousness. Upon his neurological examination and CT scan, we determined that a closed head injury had occurred. All of your actions have increased the chances of Earl experiencing a full recovery. On our part, surgery was done to repair the skull. Most people who have had this type of head injury experience no lasting consequences. Earl will be observed in the hospital for a brief amount of time and then he can most likely resume normal activities in a few days. "Do you have any questions?" the doctor asked.

"We just want Daddy to be okay. When can we see him?" Delta questioned.

"I see no reason why you could not go back for a short visit, and the emphasis is on shortness," said the doctor.

As the three of them walked down the hospital corridors in search of Earl's bed, everyone was quiet and they dared not look at each other for fear of how ghostly they may appear. At last, they were just outside room #211 where it listed the patient as Earl Daze and then, the silence was broken.

"Mama, I think you need to go see Daddy first and Keith

and I will go in afterwards," spoke Delta, trying to be as reassuring as she could.

"Delta, I feel like I am shaking all over," spoke Mama.

"I know you feel that way, Mama, I do too, but after you see Daddy's face, you will feel much better," answered Delta as she reached over to hug Mama.

Mama slowly opened the door. As she entered the room, she could see medical equipment that she had never seen before. She gasped. There was her sweet husband with a white bandage on his head. As he turned to see who it might be, a big smile came on his face when he saw it was Pesh. It was only a few steps before Pesh was there to comfort him.

"Now, Earl, I have strict orders from the doctor that I can only stay for a short visit and I do not want you to get too excited," she said with her usual gentle tone.

Earl said, "Don't worry, Pesh, I am going to be all right. I do feel dizzy at times and my head hurts," he told her as he reached to touch the bandage on his head.

"Delta and Keith are waiting just outside the door and I know they are anxious to see you." Pesh was speaking all the while going toward the door.

"Delta, you and Keith come in here for I know you will be glad to see what I have seen," stated Pesh while reaching for Delta's arm. In no time, they were in the room.

When Delta saw her daddy, she could not get over to him quickly enough. Somehow, she missed all of the equipment Mama had seen. She just saw her loving Daddy. She put her head down on his chest and Earl took his right hand and patted her on her back.

"Delta," Daddy said, "rise up and look me in my eyes." She gently lifted her head until they were both looking directly into each other's eyes. "I love you," was all he said.

Delta broke into tears. Those words were magical and they would be the words that she would never ever forget. "I love you so much, Daddy," she told him.

They all sat down in a chair and began their visit.

"Daddy, I am so glad to see you but I will be even happier when you are home. I have been so worried about you. Why, when I came up to the barn area and saw that you were bleeding, it scared me to death. It was such a good thing that Keith dropped by when he did, or I just don't know what I would have done," Delta spoke nonstop.

"Earl, are they taking good care of you here?" Pesh asked.

"Pesh, I have been so out of it that I really can't answer that but I guess they have because I am still here," he answered her.

"Earl, you have a strong family. We have all been concerned about you," Keith spoke up.

"Keith, I need to thank you for being there for me and my family. I appreciate all you have done. When we get this all behind us, you and I need to go fishing. I think we would have a better chance of catching some fish over at Haley Lake because that pond there on the place just doesn't seem to have many fish in it. I probably need to have the thing stocked," Earl said.

All of them had such a good time visiting that they almost did not realize that the nurse had entered the room.

"I don't know what kind of party that is taking place here but visiting time is over," she forcefully said.

They quickly said their goodbyes and headed out of the door. As they reached the nursing area, another nurse stopped them.

"I know how concerned you must be for Mr.

Daze but the best thing you can do for him is to go home and get some rest." She, too, was speaking in the same tone of voice as the other nurse. "If anything changes, we have your phone number and we will give you a call," she continued, finishing up the conversation.

Although it was not an easy thing to leave Daddy they all knew they were exhausted. Not much talking was done on the trip home. They all came into the living room and collapsed in a chair.

"Delta, why don't you see when *Gunsmoke* is coming on? I know Earl will be watching it and that way we will feel like we are doing something with him here," she said with a small grin.

"Mama, *Gunsmoke* will be on in about forty-five minutes. That will give me time to find the phone number for Peggy," Delta stated.

Mama found the papers without any problem and the phone number of Delta State was also not difficult to find. But what dorm would they call to reach Peggy?

"Delta, we will have to wait until the morning to call Peggy. The phone number for the college is here; but we have to find out what dorm she is in, in order to reach her," Pesh said.

"Another thing to add to the morning's list; anyway, I dread that conversation, Mama. You know Peggy is going to be upset but do not know what to do. She will want to be with Daddy but she will not want to miss her classes. Anyway, Mama, what can she do? We are here and even we do not know what to do, yet." Delta remarked.

"Well, that may very well be the case but Peggy has a right

to know. In the morning that will be one of our tasks and that is all that needs to be said about it," Mama said as she left to try to watch *Gunsmoke*.

"Come on Delta, *Gunsmoke* is coming on," Mama insisted.

Sure enough, the sun came up the next morning. The smell of the biscuits and bacon cooking woke Delta from a sound sleep. Pesh had already fed the animals and was within minutes of waking Delta.

"Mama, you should have gotten me up sooner. We need to get to the hospital and to bring Daddy home," Delta yelled out from her room.

"Young lady, there is no need to yell," Pesh responded sharper than she intended.

"I am sorry, Mama. I am just nervous about Daddy. Will you please forgive me for I know you have to be feeling worried too?" she responded.

"Yes, there is enough worry to go around, I guess. Sit down at the table and I will get you a couple of biscuits and some bacon," Mama replied with her usual smile.

Both of them knew how much love there was between them and that because of Daddy's accident their nerves were frayed.

"Delta, it is time for us to call the college. Will you please find out how we reached Peggy?" Mama said as she sat down in the chair close to the phone.

Delta dialed Delta State and the operator answered. Delta cleared her throat. "Good morning, my name is Delta Daze and my family, I, have a sister attending college there. Her name is Peggy Daze. There has been an accident involving our daddy and we need to talk to her," Delta stated.

"Just a moment, please, and I will send your call to the Dean's Office. They will be able to help you," the operator said.

About thirty seconds passed before Delta was speaking to the Dean. The Dean informed them that Peggy Daze was in Dorm D and she gave them the direct phone number for the dorm.

By this time, Delta was getting a little nervous as to what to say because she knew how upsetting this would be to her sister. Her hands were shaking as she dialed the number. Again, she was received by a nice lady. She asked Delta for the phone number for Peggy to return the call because Peggy was already in class. Without hesitation, Delta gave her the number.

"Mama, we are going to have to wait for Peggy to call us. She is in class but the lady assured me that she would get the message and have her give us a call," Delta said and then left the room to do the things she needed to do.

"Mama, I hear Keith driving up. Are you ready to go?" Delta questioned.

Delta was so undone with the whole situation; she did not even listen for a response because she was on her way to open the door for Keith.

"I am so glad to see you. Come on in here. Have you had breakfast?" she asked.

"Delta, slow down because you are nervous as a cat in a room full of rockers," he said with a laugh.

"That line is as old as these hills. I am just anxious to get Daddy home. I know he wants out of that hospital. Why, you know how Daddy is about those places. You should, you know, you talk to him enough," she said.

"I know that but the doctors have not said that he can come home until he has been checked out. Anyway, Mama Pesh may not even be ready yet. I think I will have some of her biscuits, and some honey to go with them," he told her all the while walking toward the kitchen.

Just about that time, Pesh walked into the room. "Keith, do not let her rush us. We know that hospitals don't get in a hurry and, it is just as you said, nobody has said that today is the day that he is coming home. Delta just has it in her head that everybody works according to her timetable and they just do not," Pesh said, handing him a plate with several biscuits. "Now, if it is honey that you want to go with the biscuits then you will have to reach over to the cabinet behind you to get it. I will get you the butter." Pesh told him.

Keith was so used to this family's matter-of-fact attitude that these kinds of things never fazed him.

Mama was cleaning the kitchen when the phone rang.

"Delta, will you please get that? It is most likely Peggy," Mama said. She left the room to go where the phone was.

"Hello, this is Delta speaking," she said.

"Hi, Delta, what is going on? I know you would not call me at college just to talk. Please tell me?" Peggy asked.

"Peggy, Mama asked me to call you to let you know that Daddy has been in an accident. He is in the hospital now but we are hoping that Dr. Smith will release him today. We were with him yesterday. He had surgery to keep the skull bone that was broken from moving. We visited him in the room and, although his head was hurting, which is understandable, he talked to us until the nurse made us leave. It seems as though he is going to get well under the care of the doctor and his family," Delta spoke, nonstop almost without a breath between sentences.

After talking with Delta and Mama, it was decided that Peggy should remain at college and they would call her if anything changed. Otherwise, Peggy is to call in three days just to, hopefully, talk to Daddy.

They all loaded into Keith's car and were off to, hopefully, to bring Earl home from the hospital. It was not long before they were pulling into the parking lot. Keith opened the car door for the ladies. He was always a gentleman. This time, they knew exactly where to go and it could not have come about any better if they had planned it, for there outside Earl's room stood his doctor.

This time Delta was not one bit bashful. She walked right up to the doctor ready to question him.

"Dr. Smith, are you going to let Daddy come home today?" she asked.

"Good morning, everyone. I have just examined Earl and it does appear that he is doing very well, so I see no reason, if there is someone there to care for him, that he cannot be released today," was his reply.

It did not take any time for that news to register with Delta. She left Mama and Keith to finish up with the doctor.

Earl's hospital door flew open with the homecoming news being excitedly shared by Delta. "Daddy, I just knew you would be coming home today and I am so glad. I know you want out of this place. How are you feeling? I told Mama and Keith that you will be coming home but they did not believe me. They told me that I thought that all things should be done my way," she just kept talking and Daddy was just listening and enjoying it.

She was as happy as he had ever seen her. There are so many good things to remember about my two daughters. I love them so much, he was thinking.

"Delta, please hand me my shirt. I need to get dressed so we can head home. I know it has not been that long but I sure will be glad to sleep in my bed. I need to check on Queen," he said.

Delta quickly spoke up, "Oh, no you are not going to do any such thing. You are going home to rest and let us take care of you. The doctor told us that is what we are supposed to do. Now you are tramping all around in the pasture and barn seeing after some horse. It is just not going to happen, Daddy," Delta spoke up.

"I know, Delta; but it is a difficult thing to just sit around and let others wait on you," Daddy replied in a disappointed tone. "Pesh, it sure feels good to be home. I missed you. Did you happen to watch *Gunsmoke* last night? It sure was a good show. Old Matt has to keep Chester on the straight and narrow but he can be so funny at times. I thought about all of you as I was watching it," he said as he reached over to give her a hug.

"Yes, we did see the show and we thought of you every minute of it," Pesh replied.

"Keith, pull up a chair and make yourself at home," Earl told him.

"Daddy, I am going to go fix us some tea," Delta said as she left the room.

"Earl, I am going to go get you that nice comfortable pillow you love," Pesh told him.

It was not long before Delta was passing out the tea to everyone and they all settled in to, hopefully, learn what Earl could remember about the accident.

"Daddy, we want to know what you remember about the day your accident happened," Delta questioned.

"Well, child, things were a bit fuzzy for me a couple of days after the accident but I believe I have pieced it together as to what happened the day of my accident," Earl spoke in a strong voice.

All of them were listening with all ears. To be more comfortable, Earl placed the pillow behind his back and began his story.

"The day started out just fine. The sun was shining bright and there was a comfortable breeze in the air, so I thought I would sit out on the porch for a while, so I did. I picked my stick up to whittle for a bit and then I heard Queen talking near the barn. Well, you know me; I began to think that she must need something. That old horse doesn't just talk for nothing and I want her to be happy, you know that, Delta. As I headed down the hill, I stopped to speak to our neighbor but it was not long before I was opening the gate to the pasture. Now, mind you, Queen was still talking so I picked my pace up. Well, there she was in front of the barn, just standing there. I checked her water; it was just fine. I checked her feed; it was just fine. So, I shook my head questioning just what all the commotion was about and just about that time, an old green snake came slithering from the grass. It was just a garter snake, so I was not at all afraid. Just as I reached down to pick the dang thing up, Queen raised her feet in the air. Well, you see, it must be that somehow her knee caught me in the head because that is the last thing that I remember," he spoke with confidence.

"Delta, can you come in here?" Pesh called out.

Only about thirty seconds had passed before Delta was there. "You called me, Mama. I was in the kitchen putting up the dishes this morning. Daddy, is there anything that I can get you? I want you to be comfortable," she said.

"No, child, I feel pretty good right now. Maybe later I will need you to help get me positioned in bed. I know Pesh will need help," he said.

"Delta, the reason that I called you is I need you to go up in the attic. I placed my knitting container up there out of the way a couple of weeks ago but since we are going to be inside quite a bit, I think I will do some knitting," Pesh asked.

"Sure, Mama, I will go right now," Delta quickly responded.

Delta went to the cabinet to get the flashlight and made her way toward the attic. Their attic was always well organized, both Earl and Pesh saw to that. Walking into the attic, Delta decided to just take a look around. Just look, over there is my doll. She strolled over to pick the doll up. She dusted it off and memories began to flood her mind. I remember when I used to rock you to sleep. I think your name is Lucy. We had some good times together. I know that you did not cry or do some of those fancy things other dolls could do but that did not matter. Peggy and I used to play house and you were always such a good baby. Peggy had a baby that cried a lot, no real crying, but you know what I mean. She was having fun just remembering those times when she was quickly brought back to reality by hearing Mama, just underneath the stairs. I had better find that knitting thing before Mama calls me, she thought.

Delta saw that Mama was in the kitchen. "I found it, Mama, without much trouble," she said, handing the container over to Mama.

"Thank you for going up there for me. I just can't get up

there as easily as you can," Pesh said.

"No problem, Mama, I would like to help you fix something for supper, if you will let me?" Delta asked.

"For sure, I can use the help. Would you get some potatoes and peel them? I want to have some mashed potatoes. Earl loves them," she requested.

"Mama, I have been reading about some ways that can help Daddy recover. Do you think Daddy would mind if I shared them with him?" Delta asked.

"No, not in the least do I think he would mind. I think it would please him that you cared enough to read about ways that can help him get over this," Mama said to her.

While Mama was finishing up supper, Delta took the opportunity to share what she had learned.

"Daddy, I have been reading up on some things that you and we, as a family, can use to help you get better. Do you want to hear them?" she asked.

"Yes, I would," Daddy said.

"Here they are," she said as she began sharing her list.

"1st Drink at least six cups of fluids, water is best, every day for at least a week. These fluids can help reduce inflammation.

2nd Take vitamin C every day because this helps reduce inflammation, too, and helps your tissue repair.

3rd Walk at least a bit every day. I asked the doctor about this and he told me that it would be fine but he said as soon as you get tired, stop walking.

4th Don't lift anything over five pounds. Daddy, a bag of flour is five pounds.

5th Ask us for help. You should not be lifting, bending or reaching. Please don't be shy about letting us help you because that is what family is here for and we will be glad to help you.

Remember the old saying, Daddy 'pay a little now, or you will pay a lot later'," she stated and gave a big smile and a wink to her daddy.

Chapter Eighteen

Keith Makes Marriage Plans

A week had passed since Keith had learned about the baby. It was on his mind almost all day and night. Here, it was Sunday night once again and he knew what his heart felt and wanted to do. He had talked to Delta almost every day and he wanted to go with her on her next doctor's visit. She had told him it would please her.

The next morning things began at the Stone farm as every morning had since the day Keith was born, with the rooster crowing at the top of his lungs. Keith wiped the sleep from his eyes and immediately his brain went to what he had been told the week before. He went to the bathroom to shave, shower, and get dressed. As he looked into the mirror, he knew exactly what he wanted to do.

Arriving at the kitchen, he could smell the wonderful aroma of Katie's biscuits and bacon ready to eat. Bobby and Katie were already sitting at the table.

"Dad, you know that tract of land I have always had my eye on to one day built a house on," Keith opened without so much as a good morning. When he realized it, he corrected himself. "I am sorry, good morning, Mama and Daddy."

"Good morning to you, Son," Katie quickly spoke.

"Same here, Son and, yes, I know exactly the land you

speak of. Why do you ask?" Bobby questioned.

"I want to start building a house on it," Keith firmly said, "and the sooner I get started the better. What do we need to do to get started?" he questioned as though his dad had already approved it.

"Son, you just keep talking without waiting for an answer from me and your Mama as though we have already given you the go-ahead," Bobby spoke with intensity.

"I'm sorry, ya'll, but I just have always thought that this land would one day be mine and I feel like that day has come," Keith replied.

Bobby arose from the table, walked over to the coffee pot, and poured him some coffee. "Would anybody like some more coffee?" he questioned.

Katie replied, "No, thank you."

Keith said, "No, thank you, Dad, I have not started the first one."

"Son, why are you in all such a rush now on building a house? Are you not pleased living here?" Bobby questioned.

Katie felt the need to speak up. "Have we done something to offend you, Son?" she asked.

"No, Mama, no one has offended me. If the two of you must know, I plan on asking Delta to marry me. That is why I would like the land to build a house for us and our family," Keith said as he stood as if ready to defend himself.

"Marry, Katie said, you have not known this young lady that long. How long, three months? Yes, she appears to be a nice person, but to marry so soon?" she questioned.

"Mama, how long do you think I need to know her? I love her, can't both of you understand that?" Keith's voice had now risen to a higher level.

"Okay, son, there is no need to be upset. Let's talk this thing out reasonably," Bobby told him.

Keith was now pacing the floor as he turned to address the issue. "You are not going to change my mind. I am twenty-five years old. I believe I know my own heart. I have given this a lot of thought. Do you two believe that I do not know, in my own heart, what I want, or who I want? Goodness gracious you did not do this kind of interrogation when John told you he was going to join the U.S. Army. What kind of danger do you think I am getting into by marrying the woman I love?" he asked.

"Son, the two things cannot be compared. Yes, John came in and discussed his decision and we agreed, but marriage is a totally different thing. It is a lifetime commitment," Bobby replied.

By this time, Katie was standing up. The only one still seated was Bobby. Katie needed to have some answers, so she asked, "When are you planning on asking her, or have you already asked her?"

"No, Mama, I have not yet asked her but soon I will. Okay, you do not have to give me the land. I just have always thought that it was going to be mine, with only the asking," Keith said.

"Keith, the land can be yours. All we have to do is go to a lawyer and have it deeded over to you. That's all," Bobby told him.

Keith sat down by his dad and asked, "So, you will deed the land to me, so I can start my house?"

"Yes, I will start on it today. Do you agree, Katie?" Bobby asked.

"I do not have a problem with the land. It is the marriage that I question. The girl has not even been to this house for as much as a visit," Katie replied, now almost in tears.

"Mama, I do not want to see you upset like this. Delta is a fine young lady and there are no finer people than her mama and daddy. I will bring her over so you and Dad can see for yourself how fine she is. Though, Mama, you are not the one marrying her, I am, please see that because I am going to ask her. You cannot change my mind," by this time Keith was looking directly into Katie's eyes as he spoke.

Keith did not wait for a negation. He was tired of trying to make them understand and, of course, just the mention of the baby would have sent them into orbit. He reached for his hat and went out the back door to his car. Usually, he would be asking what needed to be done on the farm but the farm was the last thing on his mind. It was Delta he was concerned about.

He arrived at the Daze house, without even calling first. Manners were out the window right now because he needed to see Delta. He did take time to stop in town at the jewelry store to buy a ring. It was not an expensive one for he knew he needed most of the money in his savings for the building of the house. He knew Delta would understand that. But the big question was would she agree to marry him?

While knocking at the door, he could feel his stomach churning. Would she say yes, or no? Ms. Pesh came to the door.

"Good morning, Keith, we were not expecting you," she softly spoke.

"Good day to you, Ms. Pesh and I apologize for not calling first but I need to see Delta. Is she here? I will give her time to get ready. I don't mind waiting in the car," he said/

"Oh my, you do not need to do that. You come on in and

sit down and I will get you something to drink or eat, just whatever you want. I believe Delta will need a bit of time to prepare for your visit but I know that she will be glad to see you," Pesh told him all the while directing him to a chair in the dining room.

"Thank you kindly but I have had my breakfast, along with a lot of talking with my folks. They know I am here and they know why," Keith replied, feeling like he was giving too much information away, for he was not sure what Delta had even said to her or Mr. Earl about him knowing about the baby.

In his head he thought, now that is stupid. It would take a blind man not to know about the baby. Maybe he had noticed that Delta was putting on some weight but his thoughts were always just about being with her. Reality quickly drew him back to the moment.

"I am sorry, Ms. Pesh but my mind is going ninety miles a minute. I do not intend to be rude. I will just wait here for Delta, if you don't mind."

Leaving the room, Pesh could probably guess that Delta already knew that Keith was here but she headed for her bedroom anyway.

"Yes, Mama, I know Keith is waiting. Please tell him that I will be right there," Delta said feeling as if her heart was in her throat.

The two of them had spoken over the phone every day since their trip to Shiloh and he was always such a gentleman. In her heart, she knew she should not be so nervous. She straightened her hair, put on some lipstick, and added just a little cologne. She had on a beautiful blue Swiss-dotted top and blue jeans which looked great on her. Taking one last look in the mirror, she turned to go into the dining room.

Keith stood up when she walked into the room. Wow, as always, she looked beautiful. There was no one he would rather spend his life with.

"Hi, Delta," he greeted her.

"Good morning, Keith, you may sit down. You are out early today but I am glad to see you," she replied.

"I was wondering whether you would take a drive with me?" he asked. "I hope you will say yes."

"I would love to but let me tell Mama," and as she said that, she left for the kitchen since she was sure Mama was in there washing dishes.

"Keith, do you know how long we will be?" she asked. Mama wants to know.

"I would love for us to have some lunch in town and then I have somewhere special I want to take you. Ask Ms. Pesh is two o'clock too late?" he replied.

"Two is fine she says."

Delta was feeling great today. She was, without a doubt, wondering what Keith had on his mind.

"It is a beautiful day," she opened the conversation as they drove toward town.

But just as they got closer to Coldwater, Keith turned toward Independence where their farm was.

"Are we going to your house?" she questioned.

"In a way," Keith said as he grinned at her.

He was so excited to let her know what was on his mind. There was a road that led directly up to the acres where he wanted to build their house. He stopped the car.

"I've been here before. This is your land," she said.

"You are right in some ways," was his reply.

He went to the other side of the car, opened the door, and

172

got down on one knee. His hands were shaking as he pulled the small blue box from his pocket.

"Delta, I know that I do not have a lot of money but I have enough to get us a house started and maybe almost complete." He opened the box. The small diamond glistened in the sunlight. "I want you to be my wife. Please, will you do the honor of marrying me?" he asked.

Delta was so moved. Keith was one of the finest men she had ever known and she knew he had given this a lot of thought, but she still had some questions.

"Keith, you are not doing this just because of the baby, are you?" she asked.

"No, Delta, I love you and I believe I have from the very first time I laid my eyes on you. Now, this baby will be our baby and I promise you, I will love him or her with all my heart and do my very best to provide all I can for the three of us. Education will be very important and knowing God, the most important. This child will be in my heart just as much as if it was mine. Then when the time is right, you and I can have more children, that is if God sees fit to give us more. Delta, will you marry me?" he asked again.

"Yes, Keith, I will marry you, but we have to talk to Mama and Daddy," she added.

"Oh, without question we will," he agreed and then he placed the ring on her finger.

"How would you like to get married in October?" he questioned.

"That sounds like a fine month to me. Now, what date would we like? What about October 14th? That is a Friday night," he added.

"If Mama and Daddy and your parents do not have a

problem with it, then October 14ᵗʰ we will get married," she said as she reached out of the car and grabbed him by the neck; then they kissed.

"As soon as my parents deed the land to me, I will start on building our house. I want some of the ideas you have before I have the plans drawn up," he said with great joy in his eyes. "Then there is, of course, the approval of my parents deeding the land to me."

"Why, I thought they considered it your land?" Delta asked.

He quickly replied, "Oh, I do not anticipate a problem." He did not let her know of the earlier conversation he had with his parents. Honestly, he did not know how his parents were going to react when he told them that Delta was pregnant. "I will take care of that; you just don't worry your pretty head about that. We have got to leave now and take you by the doctor's office to make sure everything is okay with you and the baby."

They drove into Dubbs. Fortunately, there was only one patient there to see the doctor. It was not long before the nurse called for Delta to step back into the examination room.

She appeared a little nervous. Keith could sense it and tried to reassure her that everything was going to be fine.

Doctor Leake asked him to return to the waiting room until the exam was finished and then he would call him back. There was no hesitation on Keith's part.

"Well, Ms. Daze, how have you been since I saw you last?" the doctor questioned.

"Sir, I do not know of a problem," she quickly replied.

The doctor called his nurse in so that he could examine her. Pulling the gloves off, he informed her, "Delta, the baby is growing just fine and no problem was detected. I want you to return in one month."

Delta straightened her clothes and returned to the waiting room where she informed Keith of the good news.

"Oh, I wish I knew if we were having a girl or boy," she said.

"Now, Delta, we will be happy with either one. You know that," he answered.

Delta stared at the beautiful engagement ring on her finger. She felt so very blessed to be marrying Keith but she could not help but be concerned as to how his parents were going to react to the baby. She wished with all her heart that she did not, once again, have to go into the rape. She would rather forget about it and going over it only brought back all of the pain. However, she knew the truth was always better than a lie. Maybe it is best if I just leave this to Keith to explain to them; if I have to go into the details, then I will have no choice because they have a right to know.

They arrived back home at the time they had told Pesh to expect them.

"I will not go in, Delta, for I have to go talk to Dad and Mom about the land, but let your folks know that it was good to see them."

Before leaving, he placed his hand on her belly. Delta knew that he was saying that he loved the baby and that made her feel so good inside.

Chapter Nineteen

Trouble at Home for Keith

Driving home, Keith could not help but think about how he was going to let his folks know about the baby. He, too, did not want to discuss the rape for he did not want to put Delta through that ordeal. *How should I handle this?*

As he entered the house, he could smell supper cooking; he was hungry, too. He saw Katie at the stove and immediately went over and kissed her on the cheek.

"Hi, Mom, how was your day?" he asked.

"I have been pretty busy working on a quilt today. Might I ask what you have been up to?" she asked, dreading the answer for she believed it would have something to do with Delta Daze. "I gather you went to see Delta."

"Yes, I did. I asked her to marry me. I do not want to go over this another time so we had better get Dad in here for the discussion," he insisted.

"Son, do you want to eat supper first?" she asked.

"If you would rather, then that is fine with me, but we are going to discuss this tonight, for sure," Keith firmly answered.

He did not feel like he was a boy any longer; he wanted his parents to respect him as a man and therefore respect his decisions.

Supper was delicious as always. The three of them left the

kitchen for the living room. After each was comfortable and Katie had finished pouring the coffee, Keith opened the conversation.

"Dad, as I told Mom, I asked Delta to marry me. I took her over to the land where I want to build our house and that is where I proposed to her. She said yes," Keith voiced with confidence.

"Well, I guess she did," Katie quickly replied.

Keith took offense to her reply. "Now what do you mean by that, Mom? Delta could have any man in this county or state, for that matter. I am honored that she said yes."

"Okay," Bobby spoke up, "let's all stay calm and not get upset. We are family and we need to act like one."

"Then both of you need to realize that I am old enough to know who I want as my wife and respect that. I know that ya'll don't know Delta but when you do, you will love her because she is a fine young lady," he seemingly pleaded.

"I just wish you would wait some time longer, for there is no rush. You can do things together and get to know each other better is what I recommend," Katie stated.

Keith could not stay seated any longer. He walked as if he was going out the door and then turned and stated, "Delta is pregnant."

By this time, Katie and Bobby were on their feet. "What did you say? Pregnant!" Katie exclaimed as if she heard wrong.

Bobby said nothing.

"Yes, you heard me right. The baby is due in December and we would like to get married in October, October 14th, as a matter of fact."

"Son, I thought I had raised you boys better than that. I

would have believed you would have respected a young lady enough to wait until your wedding night to do such a thing," Bobby spoke with disappointment in his voice. "Then what about her, why would she allow this?" he asked. By this time, he was seated with his head in his hands. This conversation was not at all comfortable.

Then Katie quickly said, "Young man, you can just forget about that land. We will never deed the land to you. How could we now?"

"You could, just like you have always led me to believe that it was mine. That is how. How does our baby change my having the land? he asked with confusion.

Katie answered, "It is not the baby. It is the whole situation. Can you not see that?"

"No, I cannot see that. What I see is that I love Delta, she loves me, and we are having a baby, period. That is all there is to it, Mom."

Keith was getting nervous now because he knew what they were thinking. Honestly, he did not care if they thought he and Delta had conceived the baby; whatever they said, it was not going to change his mind about marrying her.

"Okay, don't deed me the land. I will buy some land from someone around here. I know I can get the financing. It will take me longer to pay off my house but that's okay. I can do this without your damn piece of land," he spoke harshly.

Without waiting for a response, he grabbed his hat and went out the back door.

Bobby and Katie looked at each other in total astonishment. What had they done? It was very true that even as a young boy Keith had always had his heart set on that acreage of land, and now they felt as if they had reneged on their word. What right did they have to tell him who to marry, especially now that she was having his child, their grandchild?

Bobby spoke up first. "Katie, I believe that we are wrong for the way we are handling this. We know we have raised a good young man. He has always been devoted to helping me on the farm without so much as a complaint, that I can remember. He has a heart of gold when it comes to caring for others. I just know, in a second, he could go to Mama, and she would not hesitate to deed him any piece of her property that he wanted and probably help him in the building of the house. You know she loves him that much and you know how much he loves his grammy. I can only imagine what she would say or think about us doing this to Keith. You know, John will expect some acreage to build a house when he returns from the Army, that is if he comes back here to live, which, of course, may not happen. Nevertheless, if he did, would we not give it to him? Katie, I am afraid we could be being unfair to our son. Do you not have the same concerns?" he asked.

By this time, Katie had tears running down her cheeks. She could hardly speak but she nodded her head in confirmation.

"Excuse me, I need to go to the bathroom, Bobby," she told him as she practically ran out of the room. There, she stood and wept. It was a good fifteen minutes before she felt like returning to pick up where they had left off.

Katie started off the conversation as she asked, "Bobby, there is something about this young lady that I am remembering. It was the time that Ginny was in the hospital with pneumonia that has come to mind. There was a knock on Ginny's hospital room door, and when I opened the door, Delta was standing there. After our introduction, she said that she

179

had come to visit Mrs. Stone. She had a book in her hand which she brought to read to Ginny. You know, she did not have to do that. It was a kind gesture on her part, and one I believe is important in showing us her character. Bobby, do you think that we should invite Delta over here soon for supper? If we do that, I believe we will get to see what exactly Keith has seen in her," Katie stated. "We have to face the facts, a girl does not get pregnant without help, so we can't just blame her. I love my son and I want to know my grandchild. You are absolutely right when you say that Keith's grammy would step in and help him in a heartbeat."

"Well, it is settled. In the morning, we will ask Keith to invite Delta over for supper on Friday night and then we will let him know our decision," Bobby instantly agreed.

They both felt like a weight had been lifted off their shoulders, although Keith had no idea of their resolution.

Keith had no idea where he was going, he was just going. He could not remember when he had ever been this upset with his mom and dad.

One thing was certain, as soon as he could get together with Delta, he would find out exactly who knew about the father of the baby. He did not like misrepresenting folks but as far as he was concerned, he would be the father of the baby and no one needed to know any difference. He did not care if they judged him for having intercourse before marriage, for the baby was far more important than any old reputation. Let people think what they will for they will anyway.

As a matter of fact, Keith continued in thought, we do not need to wait until October to get married. If Delta would agree to it, they should get married soon, and that was what he intended on proposing to her.

By the time Keith arrived back home, his mom and dad had already gone to bed. Believing they would most likely be asleep, he thought it best to wait until morning to have any further conversation.

As the sun rose from the east, the rooster quickly began crowing. Keith stared up toward the ceiling, wondering how the day would end. How should he approach Mom and Dad in just a short while? Would Delta agree to marry right away? There were so many questions whirling through his mind that he could hardly think straight. But he better get dressed and face whatever the outcomes might be.

Bobby and Katie were, as usual, already seated at the table for breakfast. Keith was, in most cases, the last one to arrive.

"Good morning, Mom and Dad," he said with a smile. It was almost as if nothing had taken place the night before.

"Good morning to you, too. How did you sleep?" Katie spoke up first.

"Same here, Son. Do you mind if I ask where you went last night?" Bobby questioned. He glanced over to Katie because he knew she was also wondering whether he had visited Grammy.

"I just drove around thinking. That is all," Keith answered.

Bobby opened the discussion. "After you left, Katie and I thought it would be a good idea to invite Delta over for supper on Friday. What would you say about that?" he asked.

"Sure, I think she would like that, but I do not want you to show her any disrespect about the pregnancy. I will ask her if she can come; I am sure she wants to see you. Once again, I warn you to watch any disrespectful statements," he emphasized with an unyielding spirit.

Katie could understand why he was feeling this way so she tried her best to reassure him. "Keith, we honestly want to get to know her. She will be our daughter-in-law and soon give birth to our first grandchild. We will be kind. We promise you."

Bobby wanted to add his reassurance so he said, "Keith, during her visit, we will be on our best behavior, We would like to discuss the land you want to have deeded to you; that is if you still want it?"

Bobby smiled when he said this with the hope that his son would know that they had quite possibly overreacted the night before and had his best interests at heart.

Keith began speaking. "Dad, unless you have something urgent that needs taking care of, I would like to call Delta to see if she has some time for me this morning."

"No, go right ahead. I will be fine with the things I have planned to work on this morning but I will need you later this afternoon."

"I got you, Dad," he said and with that, he grabbed two biscuits and sausage. Then he grabbed his hat and it was in no time that they heard the old back door slam.

Thirty minutes later, Keith pulled into the Daze's driveway. Mr. Earl was outside working on a tractor.

"Morn, sir," Keith shouted as he headed toward the front door. Only this time, he got lucky because Delta answered the door. She looked radiant. She was wearing a yellow top with white pants and had a yellow ribbon in her hair.

"You sure do look pretty; then again, you always do," Keith said without hesitation. "Are you sure you can always be with me for a short while?" he asked.

"Keith, my man, I would be happy to go with you but as

you know, I must tell you-know-who."

As they were driving along, Keith told her that he had something to ask her. "Will you come to supper at our house on Friday night upon Mom and Dad's invitation?" he asked, giving her his beautiful smile.

"I would be happy to come. Oh, Keith, I hope they like me and, oh my goodness, the baby. What have you told them about that?" she questioned.

Keith wanted her undivided attention so he stopped the car at a roadside park so they could talk. "Listen, I need to know who knows the identity of the father of your child; give names, please."

Delta cocked her head to one side, placed her finger on her chin and began telling him the list of names, "Mama, Daddy, Peggy, Agnes, Barbara, Bill Lawson, Sheriff Miller, Dr. Leake, and you. That's it, why?"

Keith wanted to be as serious as he could possibly be so he made sure he had her undivided attention as he spoke. "You and I are going to get married and I was thinking last night that there is no reason that we should wait until October. Let's get married soon. We do not need all that celebration stuff; we just need each other to get married. If you have to live at home for a while, as maybe I will, then that will not matter either. Also, and this is the most important thing, I do not like to seem deceptive but there is no reason whatsoever why anybody else needs to know how this baby was conceived. The baby will be mine, period. I do not care about reputation. Delta, folks are going to think and say whatever they will and I don't care. I just care about you and our baby. What do you think? Now, you know that will include my folks — they are not to know."

"Well, I hate to make a decision on getting married

without letting Mama and Daddy in on it but after that, let's do it." As she spoke these words, she grabbed him in a tight embrace.

"I am the luckiest person alive to have found you, Keith Anderson Stone, and as far as I am concerned, you are this baby's father."

"Oh, I get the whole name treatment," he replied as he held her tightly, giving a chuckle.

Delta thought of the dress she wanted to wear and then all of the planning began. Keith just sat back and enjoyed listening to her. His heart could not be any fuller with love, both for her and the baby. Honestly, he could not wait to hold the little one in his arms.

"Look, if you can stop planning long enough, here is what I would like for us to do. We will have supper at my house on Friday night and then on Saturday morning, let's be ready to leave for a town just across the Alabama State Line. There, you do not have to have a blood test or a waiting period and we can get married sometime after lunch. Do you think you can fit all of your plans in a suitcase?" he joked, looking cross-eyed at her with a big grin.

"Wow, that will be quick! I hope I have a suitcase that big," she replied in the same manner, cross-eyed and with a big grin.

"Then it is decided so I will start on plans to map it all out. The best town and way to go is something I still need to figure out. I will have it all done by Friday night," he promised.

Friday night came so quickly. Delta was feeling nervous because meeting Keith's parents was only a few hours away. It is exciting and disconcerting, both, for they are going to be in her life as in-laws and grandparents to their baby, she thought. She wanted so much to make a favorable, no, a great impression on them.

A few negative thoughts floated through her brain. What will be their reaction when they see me with my big tummy? Are they thinking that Keith and I have already had intercourse? Well, of course they do, how else could there be a baby. Oh, heavens, what do they think about that? Before long, tears dropped from her eyes onto her belly. As she reached down to wipe them, the baby moved with greater strength than he or she ever had, as if to let her know to stop thinking negatively.

"Little one, it is going to be Keith, you, and I, and that is all that matters. I love you so much."

Keith arrived right on schedule. She wore a lovely red blouse along with blue pants. Peggy had fixed her hair up in a French twist and it looked so pretty.

She gave Keith a quick kiss and began the conservation. "I would be lying if I did not admit to you how nervous I am and have been all day."

"Delta, you have nothing to be nervous about. My folks don't bite." He could not help but laugh out loud. "Just listen to this music; that should calm your nerves," he said, trying his best to be serious. "They are just people like your people so just be your lovable self and you haven't a single thing to be concerned about."

Chapter Twenty

Delta and Keith Are Getting Married

Delta and Keith had secured all of the blessings of anyone that was important to their union and now their big day was close at hand. There was no denying that Delta was very pregnant so waiting just did not seem like an option. They had decided on September 14th as their wedding date. Twas the night before and Delta seemed more nervous than she had ever been in her life. She could not understand why. She loved Keith with all her heart and he loved her.

Peggy strolled into the room with what seemed like endless questions, "So, Sis, are you all prepared for this? What do you think your wedding night will be like?"

Delta was nervous enough and all these questions were over the top. "Peggy, stop with the questions. Don't you have something to do somewhere else in this house, not in my room?" Delta asked in a harsh manner.

Peggy got the idea and decided it best to leave Delta to her thoughts.

Delta had a beautiful white skirt and blouse pressed and ready for the day. Mama had made her a lovely bouquet of fresh flowers. It was almost time for Keith to arrive.

Their trip to Alabama would not be too long or tiring. It was getting more difficult for Delta to ride long distances so she certainly hoped that this trip was a short one. She had never been to Alabama but she had all confidence in Keith for he was very caring when it came to making sure she was comfortable.

Delta heard Keith knock on the front door and Daddy greeted him with his normal welcoming self. He always seemed to enjoy talking to Keith and the subject did not really matter.

Delta stepped out of her room and immediately, Keith stood up. She declared that his mouth flew open.

"Delta, you look so beautiful," Keith spoke, almost losing awareness of Earl and Pesh being in the room.

My attention quickly turned to Mama. I reached to hug her and I could feel the love shining from her eyes. We both knew the depth of our love. Words really did not need to be spoken.

Turning from Mama, there was my sweet, wonderful Daddy with tears welling up in his eyes.

"My Delta, you are so deep in my heart. I am confident that you will be marrying one of the best men that I know, if not the best. He will take great care of you and our little one. You will be away for a couple of days and then, you will come back here for a while. You will live here until Keith completes the building of your house. He prefers it that way and it is certainly okay with us. Delta, you will leave here as our youngest daughter but you will return as a young woman," he said as he hugged her ever so tightly.

Keith took my suitcase and we departed for the car. The trip would take about three hours so we needed to get started. It was a beautiful fall day and the air was crisp. It was the perfect day for our wedding.

We arrived in Florence, Alabama at about a quarter to two.

Keith knew exactly where the Justice of the Peace was located. We signed all the necessary papers. The Justice asked Keith to repeat after him.

Keith looked directly into my eyes and said, "I, Keith Anderson Stone, take you, Delta Kathaleen Daze, to be my lawful wedded wife."

The ceremony was complete.

Certainly, the ride down was a lot longer but that was okay. It was the way we wanted it. Keith told me about a restaurant called the Southern Farm Table. He and I loved good Southern cooking, so it was a great idea. We made a toast to the love we shared and our future. We enjoyed the delicious meal and made our way to our hotel room.

Keith had made reservations at the Stricklin Hotel. It was located downtown and the room was very spacious. It was much like I had imagined.

I had brought a delicate white lace gown for tonight. When I came into the room, Keith could only hold his breath and look at me as though he had never seen me before. It did my heart good to feel the special love from this man. He stood up to reach me and ever so gently, he placed me in his strong arms. It was as if he was holding a flower. He placed me on the bed and began to caress my body. His kisses were warm with such tenderness.

"Delta, I love you with everything in me," he whispered.

I could hardly speak. He stroked my hair and made my body yearn for his touch. He was fulfilling my every desire. I thought my heart would beat out of my chest as he gently touched my breast.

Due to my condition, I know he was being careful but I

assured him not to hesitate. Of course, I had never looked at any man's private parts; thankfully, I had never let my eyes see such a thing on the most dreadful day of my life. I was so desirous to feel Keith's manhood. What was I to do, I questioned? And, as if Keith knew, he reached down, took my hand and led it to his private parts, his manhood. I could feel my inhibitions release as I stroked and caressed him. And then, as if on cue, Keith pushes deep inside me.

We made love that night several times, each time a higher climax was achieved. All that I believed this man to be was demonstrated. I did not, nor have I since, ever doubted Keith's love for me or our baby.

Although they had only been gone one night, the family was glad to see us arrive home.

Keith had one thing on his mind; that was to take Delta to Dr. Leake to make certain that their baby was completely okay. Delta did not seem as concerned but she would certainly humor Keith, just to put his mind at rest.

"Come on, Delta, we need to hurry because we want to get to the doctor before closing time," Keith insisted.

Delta asked, "Mama, will you please put my suitcase inside my room?" It seems like we are in a bit of a hurry.

Dr. Leake reassured both the mother and father that the baby was doing just fine. "You two are going to have a healthy little one. Now, go on back home and let me close up this confounded office," he insisted.

"Delta, I would love to spend the night with you at your folk's house, but I think that I need to check in at home to be sure I am not needed for some task," Keith said.

"I understand. We will have many nights together," Delta said reassuringly.

She looked at her new husband and what a great feeling she had. He was a good, respectable man and his love for her and his child always shined through.

Delta waved bye to Keith and stepped inside the house. She couldn't help but wonder what Mama and Daddy were thinking. But hey, they know she is a married lady now!

Chapter Twenty-One

The Birth of Their Baby

Keith was spending many waking hours working on their house. He had given a lot of thought as to its design. Delta was going to love it and enjoy living there with her little family.

The days were getting closer and closer to her due date. Keith made certain that every appointment with Dr. Leake was kept, no questions asked. Delta thought it rather refreshing that Keith was so into all aspects of having their baby.

Delta, while looking out the window, found her mind wandering off. She could see Dr. Leake bring her baby to her and it was wrapped in a blue blanket.

"Oh, it's a boy, Dr. Leake!" Delta would exclaim.

"Now, wait, child, things are not always as they seem," the doctor would cautiously say.

Delta was more perplexed than ever. Don't boys always come in blue? No sooner had the thought entered her head, there was another. Delta would see Dr. Leake bring her baby wrapped in a pink blanket.

"Oh, it is a girl, Dr. Leake!" Delta would exclaim.

"Now, wait, child, things are not always as they seem," the doctor would cautiously say.

"Dr. Leake, I cannot get any more confused."

"Delta, Delta," Daddy had to say twice to bring Delta back

from her daydream.

"Yes, Daddy, I apologize. I guess I was somewhere a long way off," confessed Delta.

"I guess you were, child, but sometimes we need that little trip," Daddy said, trying to give her comfort from wherever she was.

"Keith is completing some last-minute touches down at the house and he wants me to drive you over. He is anxious for your thoughts," Daddy said with an eagerness to comply.

Their little house was intentionally nestled into the woods. It was such a charming place. At the south side of the house, there were several beautiful pin oak trees and a lovely grouping of dogwood trees just several yards away. The dogwoods would have to bloom next year for him to know exactly their color. On the north side of the yard, there were some very mature oak trees, the kind that drops acorns. To add to the beauty of the yard, there were several old beautiful Magnolia trees. Keith had worked several years on this track of land to make it this beautiful. They started at the ground and reached for the sky with their height. These were choice trees as far as Keith was concerned. To the back of the property, there were eight stately old pecan trees. Keith had worked hard to make certain that the yard was almost show-quality. There was so much to see; one would be bound to miss something.

"Delta, you should let me stop this truck," Daddy cautioned, fearing that his daughter, out of excitement, just might jump out!

"Just look, Daddy, just look over there." Delta was trying to contain her excitement.

"Delta, I am doing my best to find Keith, so as to save you some steps but if you jump out this truck while I am driving it… girl, why, I will not want to, but I will give you a spanking you will not soon forget." All the while, Daddy knew that he had hardly ever had to lay a hand on either of his two girls, much less Delta.

Finally, Daddy spotted Keith, sure enough, on the farther side of the property.

"Earl, please try to keep Delta from walking this far back on the property," Keith requested.

"You try to keep this wild bronco settled down, why don't you. This gal has my nerves just about shot. I suggest that you hurry on over here to where she is," Earl said in exhaustion.

"Keith, Keith," Delta yelled, running, yelling some, and yelling some more. "It is beautiful, so beautiful, that I can't contain myself."

"Delta, you had better or we will be back for a visit with Dr. Leake, too soon, quite possibly," Keith said quite firmly.

There seems to be no way to contain Delta. She ran and jumped into his arms like she was three years old.

"I tried to tell you, Keith, that she is wound up tighter than Dick's headband."

"Earl, is that safe to say around Delta?" Keith questioned.

"Well, I guess it is. How in the hell does Delta know anything about Dick's headband? I am not all that sure that I know." Anyway, right now, Delta is not going near that. So, we are good," Earl proclaimed.

Delta could not be happier. The house, the yard, and the land were absolutely perfect.

"Delta, you have been on your feet for far too long. Please come over and sit down on this stump. It looks comfortable," Keith pleaded.

"Okay, you two worry like two old women," Delta jabbed.

She was a little undone with their constant babying over her. She was a grown woman and could certainly take care of her body.

Delta looked down and there, covering the stump, was liquid. Oh no, she thought, my water has broken. Let's see, it is late November. I am due mid-December, so I will be two weeks early. That would be great because then the baby would be born far enough out that he or she would not be a Christmas baby. Anyway, whatever, her baby needs Dr. Leake.

Delta called out to Keith and Daddy. They had left her there on that stump in an all-right condition, but things had definitely made a change. She kept calling until finally the two of them came around the corner of the house. They both rushed over to Delta because it was obvious that something was not right.

"Ya'll, get Dr. Leake. My water has broken." Delta's voice was insistent."

"Earl, you head out to town for the doc and I will stay here with Delta," Keith pleaded.

"Yea, yea," Earl said as he hurried to the truck.

He did not believe that the old truck was quick enough to get to Dr. Leake and bring him back to help the situation. His thoughts went in hundreds of directions, many ending in the worst of hypothetical situations. Stop, he thought, you just do not need to go there. Delta is in good health and a strong young lady. There should be no problems that the doc cannot handle. He just needs to get here and soon!

Keith tried to be proactive. He gathered all of the quilts, blankets, and pillows from anywhere he could and put them inside the house. He had managed to build a fire in their new potbelly stove, so it was getting quite cozy in their new living room. He had carried Delta to the house and was trying to settle down for what could be a long night.

"Delta, I have not heard many words from you," Keith asked.

Honestly, he was truly concerned because he knew that his wife could be quite the talker; after all, she would not be a Daze if she did not like to talk. A grin came to his face. If only he had a fifty-cent piece for all the words he had heard Earl speak!

"Keith, did you say something?" Delta questioned all the while trying to roll over towards him.

"Yes, Delta, I was just checking on you, because it seemed to me that you just were not talking," Keith said in an empathetic way.

"Honestly, Keith, I must have drifted off for a bit. The light snow falling and the fact that I was looking outside to the dark sky meant that I must have dropped my concerns for a minute," she said, trying to reassure Keith that she was not worried; but she was.

"Keith, I wonder how much longer it will be before Dr. Leake and Daddy get here?" Delta asked, trying her best not to let Keith know how very concerned she was.

"Delta, you know Earl's driving, hurry is not what he does. I do not think the man knows how; but having said that, you know as well as I do, that that man would move heaven and earth to help his family," Keith responded with great confidence.

Just about that time, they both could hear vehicles pulling onto the property. Dr. Leake reached inside his truck to grab hold of his medicine bag.

"Earl, you come on. I will need you to boil some water."

Dr. Leake laughed as those words came out of his mouth.

They entered the small frame house into a very warm cozy room with what would appear to be anything that would make this birth as easy as it could be.

"First, Delta, I must remind you that you are a few weeks early. For that, I do not have the answer but we are living in the here and now, so with God's help and yours, you, my young lady, will assist me in delivering your beautiful child," he said to Delta in as positive a manner as he could under the circumstances. "Keith, you and Earl are considered on standby," Dr. Leake said as he motioned for them to just get out of the way.

The hours seemed to move too slowly as far as Delta was concerned. Why was the baby taking so long to get into a position to be born? She did not want her thoughts to get out of control but she did not know how to switch them off. I know, Keith. He has the ability to talk to me so that I can think better and not ramble on about why this and why that.

"Dr. Leake, I must see Keith," Delta insisted. "I know you have your reasons for having them where they are but I need Keith, and for that matter, my Daddy, too."

"Okay, child, I will go fetch them," the doc said as he motioned for the two anxious men to come into the room.

Keith immediately rushed to Delta. He began to stroke her hair. This was always calming for Delta. Anyway, she loved Keith's touch.

"Delta, can I get you a drink of water?" Daddy asked hesitantly.

"Sure you can, Daddy, I would love some water. I am feeling quite parched. This giving birth is somewhat tiring," Delta spoke, trying to reassure her daddy that all was going to be all right.

"Okay, fellows, I appreciate your help but Delta' is beginning to start the delivery of the baby, so I think a few is too many when it comes to this job. Anyway, I think that I have done this a time or two," Dr. Leake spoke. He motioned for the men to move back, not out of the room, just out of the way.

The baby's head was crowning which meant it would not be long before the birth, at least that would be the case, if the doc had anything to say about it.

"Okay, Delta, it is time for us to go to work," the doc said. "When I ask you to push, you push, and then we will rest a bit before the whole thing will begin once more," were Dr. Leake's words of encouragement. "We are working as a team to give you the healthiest baby possible. Now let's go, girl."

"Doctor Leake, many hours have passed. I have pushed and pushed some more. Are we close at all?" Delta asked.

Delta and Dr. Leake were exhausted but both knew that they were capable of the task at hand.

In just a moment, Dr. Leake said, "Push, Delta."

Delta pushed with all her might and out came, in the warm blanket the Doc was holding, a beautiful baby girl. Dr. Leake wrapped her up and handed her over to her mama.

Delta looked into those blue eyes and knew what she had always known; "I love you," she said as she gave her little girl a kiss. "Keith, Daddy, you both need it," Delta called.

"Keith, you go on, I need to talk about something with the Doc," Daddy said as he nudged Keith toward Delta.

Keith looked first into his beautiful wife's eyes and then into his daughter's eyes. "I love you, both," were the first words out of his mouth.

"We never for one moment doubted that," Delta said as

she placed Keith's hands on the baby's tiny heart.

"Delta, I know without question that you have a name in mind," Keith questioned, knowing he was going to get an answer.

"Yes, Keith, if you agree, the name I like is **Amber Rose Stone**; and with that, Keith agreed wholeheartedly!

End

Lightning Source UK Ltd.
Milton Keynes UK
UKHW010820240223
417588UK00001B/2